'Have dinner  Stefano aske

As he'd anticipated,
'I couldn't possibly.

'I owe you dessert.'

Liv backed towards the door. 'You don't owe me anything.'

'Is it a babysitting issue?'

'Yes.' She said the word quickly and then shook her head. 'No, actually that's not true. It's about *me*. I work. I spend time with my child. That's it. I'm just not interesting. You already know all there is to know.'

He was stunned by the completely false impression she had of herself. Why did she think she was boring?

Without speaking, Stefano took her face in his hands and brought his mouth down on hers. He kissed her slowly and confidently, holding her head exactly as he wanted it as he skillfully seduced her mouth.

Boring? She was exquisite.

Unsettled by the fierce intensity of his own response, Stefano dragged his mouth from hers.

'There's plenty that I don't know about you, Liv,' he said softly. 'But I intend to find out.'

Sarah Morgan trained as a nurse, and has since worked in a variety of health-related jobs. Married to a gorgeous businessman, who still makes her knees knock, she spends most of her time trying to keep up with their two little boys, but manages to sneak off occasionally to indulge her passion for writing romance. Sarah loves outdoor life, and is an enthusiastic skier and walker. Whatever she is doing, her head is always full of new characters, and she is addicted to happy endings.

ITALIAN DOCTOR, SLEIGH-BELL BRIDE

BY
SARAH MORGAN

⊙™ MILLS & BOON®
Pure reading pleasure™

First published in Great Britain 2008
Harlequin Mills & Boon Limited,
Eton House, 18-24 Paradise Road, Richmond, Surrey TW9 1SR

© Sarah Morgan 2008

ISBN: 978 0 263 86358 1

Set in Times Roman 10½ on 12¾ pt
03-1108-51845

Printed and bound in Spain
by Litografia Rosés, S.A., Barcelona

ITALIAN DOCTOR, SLEIGH-BELL BRIDE

CHAPTER ONE

'I'M ABSOLUTELY not getting married again. Not ever. Not in a million years. Don't even suggest it. Once was more than enough.' Liv closed the drug cupboard and stared at the bunch of glittering silver tinsel attached to the door. 'That can't stay there, Anna.'

'Of course it can. It's Christmas. I hung mistletoe there to begin with, until I realised that the only male I'm ever alone in this room with is the chief pharmacist.' Her colleague gave an expressive shudder. 'Now, stop changing the subject. You have to forget that you've been married before. Everyone's allowed one mistake in life.'

'Well, Jack was certainly that. A mistake disguised as a smooth-talking, good-looking man. On the outside he seemed entirely normal.' Liv glanced at her friend and gave a little shrug. 'Actually that's not true. His disguise was a bit thin in places. There *were* clues, it's just that I missed them. Which is the other reason I wouldn't dare to get involved with anyone again. Obviously I just see what I want to see.'

Anna frowned. 'You're *so* hard on yourself.'

'Well, that tends to happen when you've deluded yourself once.'

'It wasn't delusion,' Anna said firmly, 'it was trust. You trusted him. And he let you down.'

'It was delusion,' Liv said calmly, checking the stock of antibiotics. 'All the signs were there, but I ignored them because I just didn't want to see them. Even when Jack walked out of the delivery room saying "I can't do this", I told myself he was just talking about the stress of seeing his beloved wife in labour, whereas what he was *trying* to say was that he just couldn't "do" responsibility. He didn't want to be a father. And he didn't want to be married to me. It's just a pity for Max that he didn't make that decision a little bit sooner.' She put the boxes back on the shelf. 'Actually I don't mean that because then I wouldn't have Max and he's the best thing that has ever happened to me.'

'You're a wonderful mother and Max is a lucky boy.'

Is he?

Liv pushed through the guilt that was always pressing in on her. 'Well, I've learned to kick a football, if that's what you're saying, and I know the difference between a Lamborghini and a Ferrari but that doesn't make up for the fact that Max has a mother who works and no man in his life.'

Anna beamed at her. 'So use those tickets you won to the Snowflake Ball!'

'I'm not using the tickets.'

'Liv, it's Christmas! Time to let your hair down and party. This is a fabulous opportunity to meet someone. For goodness' sake, those tickets are like gold dust. Michelle on Paediatrics was offered a thousand pounds for hers but she refused to sell.'

'You're kidding! Who on earth was stupid enough to offer her that much money?' Liv's jaw dropped. 'Did she make a note of the name? I could sell my tickets and replace my car.'

'Why must you always be so practical?'

'Because I'm a single mother with a child of seven and responsibilities.' Liv checked the expiry date on a tube of eye ointment. 'If I'm not practical, we don't eat.'

'Has your car actually died?'

'Not yet. It likes to keep me in suspense.'

Anna waved a hand dismissively. 'Forget the car. This is London—you can always get the train. Keep the tickets and go to the ball, Cinderella.'

'Given the meagre contents of my wardrobe, that's not a bad analogy. I certainly have plenty of rags to choose from.'

Anna stood back and narrowed her eyes. 'I'd offer to lend you a dress but you're actually quite— Your boobs are—'

'Big,' Liv slotted in wryly. 'I am aware of that, actually, having had them stuck to the front of my chest for the past twenty-eight years.'

'You were born with those?' Anna started to laugh and Liv rolled her eyes.

'How did we start this conversation? It isn't as if we're not busy. There's ice on the roads and we've had three road traffic accidents in so far today. Last time I looked the waiting room was busier than the shops. *Stop* interfering in my life and go and heal the sick.'

'Only if you promise me that your New Year's resolution is to start seeing men. You don't actually have to get married—'

'That's a relief.'

'But at least go on a date. I'm worried about you. I mean…' Anna looked despairing. 'Aren't you lonely? When did you last have sex?'

'For crying out loud, Anna!' Mortified, Liv glanced over her shoulder to check that they were still the only two people in the tiny room.

'The fact that the mere *word* is enough to embarrass you tells me it's been far too long. You've been divorced for four years. It's time to get out there again,' Anna said firmly. 'If you're scared of a relationship then just have a one-night stand.'

'No way!' The thought horrified Liv. 'I hate the idea of waking up next to a man I don't know and don't care about. That just leads to misery.'

'There are two solutions to that. You can either kick him out of bed before he falls asleep or you could find a man you *do* know and *do* care about.'

'That just leads to misery, too. And anyway, I don't have the courage to take my clothes off in front of anyone.' Liv shuddered at the thought. 'And anyway, it isn't just about me. I have a little boy of seven. I don't want to trail a series of different men through his life. That's not how I want him to grow up.'

'You should be showing him that relationships are part of life, Liv. Yes, sometimes they go wrong. But sometimes they work. What message are you giving him? That love isn't worth taking a risk for?'

Engulfed by a tide of guilt and anxiety, Liv stared at her. 'You think I'm putting Max off relationships?'

'No, but I think you're so afraid of being hurt you just won't even give it a try, which is ridiculous because you're incredibly pretty and you have huge—'

'Anna!'

'Sorry. I just don't think you have any idea how gorgeous you are. Do you know what the men call you behind your back? Luscious Liv.'

'That's because they only ever see me with my clothes on. If they saw me naked, they'd be calling me Lumpy Liv.'

'You're ridiculous, do you know that? You have a fabulous figure.' Anna leaned forward and gave her a swift hug, her voice husky. 'I don't mean to nag or upset you but you're my best friend and I want you to meet someone nice. You *deserve* to meet someone nice. I wish I could buy you a night of hot sex for Christmas.'

'I don't want pity sex. I'd rather have bubble bath! It would be less embarrassing.' But Liv hugged her back, allowing herself an indulgent moment of female solidarity.

'Am I interrupting something?' A deep male voice came from behind them and Anna gave a strangled gasp and jumped back, her face scarlet.

'Mr Lucarelli! I mean—Stefano—' She cleared her throat, acting more like a student nurse than a senior sister with years of experience. 'We were just—we were…' Too embarrassed to speak coherently, she waved a hand helplessly and Liv sighed and took over.

'We were hugging,' she said calmly, desperately hoping that he hadn't overheard the conversation. 'Did you need something?'

Dark, challenging eyes settled on her face and Liv wished she hadn't drawn attention to herself.

Forcing herself to meet his gaze calmly, she tried not to notice his glossy black hair, his superb bone structure or the sensual curve of his mouth. He was indecently, impossibly handsome and Liv wondered idly how many female hearts *he'd* broken since he'd reached adolescence. They could probably be laid end to end across Europe. From the width of his shoulders to the blue-shadowed jaw, he epitomised all that it meant to be masculine.

He stood at least six feet two and the blue scrub suit encased a body that was hard and powerful. 'I came to tell you that we have transferred the patient to ICU,' he said in a cool tone. 'And I wanted to talk to you about Rachel.'

Anna immediately snapped back into her role as Sister. 'Is there a problem?'

'*Sì*, there is a problem,' he said impatiently, his eyes still on Liv. 'I don't want her working with me in Resus again.'

Anna frowned. 'She's a very good nurse and—'

'She can work with the others, but not me. She's nervous of me...' angling his arrogant dark head, he transferred the full force of his gaze to Anna '...and her nerves make her dangerous. Her hands were shaking, she dropped sterile instruments and every time I spoke to her, she jumped.'

Anna sighed. 'She's very young. You probably scared her.'

Bold brows came together in a frown. 'I didn't once raise my voice.'

'You don't need to. You're—' Anna broke off, clearly searching for a way to say what she wanted to say in the most tactful way. 'You're the senior consultant and obviously some of the more junior staff might find you...intimidating.'

'Then find me someone who isn't intimidated.' His voice was hard and tightly controlled. 'When I'm in Resus I don't want to have to be thinking about anyone other than the patient. I want the equipment in my hand, not on the floor and I expect the team around me to be completely focused and to anticipate everything.'

Anna's mouth tightened. 'So basically you want the people you work with to be able to read your mind.'

A sardonic smile touched his firm, male mouth. 'Precisely. That skill is essential to the smooth running of any emergency department. And now that we've cleared that up I'll leave you to your...' his gaze swept them both '...hug.'

Anna watched as he strolled back down the corridor towards his office. 'Great. Now he thinks we're lesbians.'

Liv let out a breath. '*Please* tell me he wasn't standing

there when you were talking about the size of my boobs and when I last had sex. Do you think he heard you saying that you wanted to buy me a night of hot sex for Christmas?'

'I'm not sure. Possibly.' Anna covered her mouth with her hand to smother the laughter and Liv gave a groan.

'OK, that's it. I resign. But only after I've killed you. I won't be able to look him in the face again.'

'I can't *stop* looking him in the face. I'm probably worse than Rachel. And you can't resign. You need the money. But remind me not to hug you in public again.' Anna frowned. 'Now he'll think I'm unavailable.'

'You are unavailable! You're happily married.'

'I know, but don't you just look at the man and think "sex"?'

'I look at him and think "trouble".' Liv pinned the keys into her pocket, trying to erase a disturbing image of shimmering dark eyes and bold male arrogance.

'I wouldn't mind getting into trouble with him. He certainly isn't afraid to speak his mind.'

'He has high standards,' Liv said firmly, 'and that's a good thing. He just won't accept anything less than the best and I like that. If I were to crash my car, he's the one I'd want treating me.'

'Now that is a terrifying thought.' Anna's expression was comical. 'Imagine, all your colleagues would see your underwear. Just for the record, if I'm ever brought in here and you have to cut my clothes from my body, I want you to make sure I'm wearing silk designer knickers and not chain-store cotton.'

'I think if you'd reached the point of needing to have your clothes cut off, the label on your knickers is going to be the least of your problems. Do you want me to check before or after I save your life?'

'You can joke, but I just know that Stefano Lucarelli dates women who wear matching silk underwear.'

'That doesn't mean he expects the same high standards from his patients,' Liv said dryly. 'Now, are you going to talk to Rachel or am I? His comment is justified, by the way. She's dreamy and needs to sharpen up.'

'Poor Rachel. He obviously chewed her up and spat her out. I'd better go and give her some sympathy.'

'She doesn't need sympathy, she needs a wake-up call,' Liv said briskly. 'She developed a crush on our Italian consultant from the moment he drove his Ferrari into the car park. If she stopped staring at him and concentrated on her work, she wouldn't drop things.'

'He *is* a little scary.'

'He is clever and efficient.'

'I'm glad you think so. Given that you respect him so much and you're indifferent to his charms, you can work with him in Resus so that solves one problem. Now, what was our other problem? Oh yes, what to do with your tickets to the Snowflake Ball.'

'I'm selling them. I have no man, no dress, no babysitter and no inclination to go to the ball. Nor do I have stepsisters, ugly or otherwise.'

'Invite Stefano Lucarelli.'

'Oh please! If I want public humiliation, I'll just strip naked. I have no intention of embarrassing both of us by issuing an invitation he will certainly reject.'

'He might not. He was looking at you.'

'He was probably wondering why someone with hips like mine hasn't gone on a diet.'

'You don't need to diet!' Anna looked at her thoughtfully. 'He noticed you, Liv.'

'Anna, he walked in while we were hugging and talking about sex,' Liv reminded her wearily. 'Of course he noticed me. It probably classes as one of the most embarrassing moments of my career.'

Anna ignored her. 'He's single at the moment, can you believe that? I don't get it. I mean, he's super-wealthy. His family owns some enormous construction business in Italy. There's no justice in the world, is there? Rich and good-looking is very unfair.'

'Anna, you're a married woman with two children.'

Anna ignored that, too. 'Apparently he was dating some glossy Italian actress but rumour has it that he ditched her because she was insisting on moving in with him. He's only been in the country for a month. He might be glad of a night out before Christmas.'

'He certainly strikes me as a man who needs help finding women.' Her tone sarcastic, Liv lifted a hand. 'Enough. End of subject. Do you and Dave want the tickets, or do I sell them?'

Rachel appeared in the doorway, her face pale. 'Ambulance Control just called and they're bringing in a man who was kicked on the rugby field. If you don't mind, I'd rather not work in Resus again today.' Her voice was high-pitched and decidedly wobbly. 'Dr Lucarelli was a bit…sharp.'

Anna straightened. 'Injuries?'

Rachel looked at her blankly. 'None. Except my pride, I suppose. I mean he was really—'

'The patient,' Anna interrupted her wearily. 'What are the *patient's* injuries, Rachel? And it's *Mr* Lucarelli, not "Dr". He's a trained surgeon. Surgeons are "Mr", remember?'

'Oh. Right.' Rachel cleared her throat. 'That patient was kicked.'

'Yes, but *where*?'

'He has breathing problems,' Rachel said vaguely and Liv gritted her teeth and handed Anna the keys to the drug cupboard.

'I'll take this one. Call the trauma team and ask Mr Lucarelli to come to Resus.'

'I'll send Sue to help you,' Anna muttered. 'Rachel, you and I need to have a chat.'

Leaving Anna to deal with the hapless Rachel, Liv pushed open the doors that led to the high-tech resuscitation room.

Always prepared for an emergency, the room was kept stocked and ready for patients and Liv was pulling on an apron and a pair of gloves when Stefano Lucarelli strode into the room.

He looked straight at her and for one brief, disturbing moment, neither of them spoke.

For sheer raw impact, she'd never met a man like him. Neither had she ever experienced the blaze of sexual awareness that suddenly flooded her body.

Mortified, she turned away quickly, her heart pounding and her face scarlet, just *furious* with herself for being so predictable. The man must be so tired of women staring at him. *It was just that stupid conversation with Anna*, she told herself crossly, pulling open a cupboard and removing the sterile pack she thought they might need.

Talking about sex had made her think about sex, and thinking about sex had made her—

Oh for crying out loud!

'Apparently the paramedics reported that the patient has some respiratory problems,' she said crisply, keeping her head in the cupboard for slightly longer than was necessary to give the colour in her cheeks time to fade, 'so I thought it might be wise to have a thoracotomy pack ready.'

'Good.' But there was a sharp edge to his voice that made her wonder whether she was about to become another casualty of his legendary high standards.

The doors to Resus flew open and the patient arrived along with the rest of the trauma team.

Swiftly and smoothly they transferred the patient onto the trolley and Stefano Lucarelli took charge, demanding silence from the entire team with a single sweeping glance.

He had presence, Liv admitted to herself, as each person around the trolley quietly busied themselves with their allotted tasks, while listening to the paramedic's handover. He was confident, but he didn't swagger like Greg Hampton, one of the more junior doctors. But neither was he as approachable like Phil, the other casualty officer who was currently looking for a vein in the patient's arm.

Working on automatic, Liv attached BP, cardiac and oximetry monitors to the patient and the paramedic collected his own equipment and left the room.

Stefano glanced at the monitor, a frown on his handsome face as he swiftly assessed the readings. 'Phil, put in two lines and send blood for immediate cross-matching. I want all clothes covering the front and sides of the chest removed.' He had an unmistakable air of authority that communicated itself to all the staff in the room and Liv cut through the man's clothing and reached for warm blankets to prevent him developing hypothermia.

'His respiratory rate is thirty-eight and it's very shallow.'

'He's in respiratory distress.' Stefano examined the man's chest and Liv noticed that Phil was watching out of the corner of his eye. Although he'd only been working in the emergency department for a few months, Phil soaked up information and never missed an opportunity to learn.

And there would be plenty to learn from Stefano, Liv thought, watching the way he examined the patient.

'There's a great deal of bruising,' she murmured, looking at the purplish marks on the man's ribs and Stefano looped the stethoscope round his neck.

'He has diminished breath sounds and decreased chest expansion.' Working with a cool, calm sense of purpose, he finished examining the man's chest. 'He has a clinically significant haemothorax. Call the trauma surgeon and ring the operating theatre co-ordinator and warn them. He might need a thoracotomy to drain it. Let's do a chest X-ray.'

The radiographer responded immediately. Like a carefully choreographed ballet, everyone worked simultaneously, carrying out his or her own clearly delineated roles.

'I need a hand here, Liv.' Phil was struggling to find a vein and Liv stepped forward to help. The more junior doctor slid the cannula into the vein and breathed an audible sigh of relief. 'OK, I'm in. Let's tape this, before we lose it.' Beads of sweat had formed on his forehead and his gaze flickered to Stefano. 'Wouldn't he have distension of the neck veins or raised jugular venous pressure if he had a haemothorax?'

'He's hypovolaemic.' Stefano's eyes stayed on the monitor. 'If you look closely at the patient, you'll see that there is a degree of tracheal deviation. Do we have two lines in, yet?'

'One. I'm just sending blood for cross-matching.'

'Get that second line in now. I need two lines before I put in a chest drain.'

Phil handed the bottle to Liv and then turned back to the patient to deal with the second IV.

'His veins are terrible,' he muttered after a few minutes. 'The first one was fine, but I've failed twice so far on this side. Do you want to have a go?'

Stefano stepped towards him. 'Turn his arm over. *Bene*. Cannula.' He held out a lean, strong hand and Liv passed him the equipment he needed, watching in silent admiration as the consultant slid the needle into the vein with no apparent effort.

He made the seemingly impossible look easy, she thought wistfully and clearly Phil thought the same thing because he shot her a rueful glance.

'The X-ray is up,' the radiographer said and they all turned to study the screen.

'There's no visible fluid level,' Phil murmured and Stefano's eyes narrowed, his gaze fixed intently on the screen.

'Because with the patient in the supine position the blood collects *under* the affected lung. If you look, you can see blurring of the hemidiaphragm contour. I'm ready to put in the chest drain.' He turned towards her. 'Liv?'

He knew her name?

Liv taped the cannula to make sure they didn't lose the second line. *Did he also know that she hadn't had sex for four years?* 'Sue will assist you with the drain.' Her hands occupied, she glanced towards her colleague. 'There's a sterile pack behind you. I got it out earlier.' Then she turned back to Phil. 'That blood needs to be given through the rapid infuser,' she reminded him. 'It needs to be warmed.'

'Sue can help Phil. I want you to assist me.' The sudden bite in his tone left no room for argument so Liv simply stepped aside so that Sue could take her place, quietly instructed her to call the operating theatre and the trauma consultant and then opened the sterile pack herself.

Suddenly she found that her hands were shaking and she shook her head, exasperated with herself. All right, so he'd already demolished Rachel—he obviously had high standards, but so did she! She had no reason to be nervous.

Working quickly, Liv opened the cannula that she knew he'd need, but he was already one step ahead, his movements so swift that it required all her concentration to keep up.

For a terrifying moment she almost lost her nerve. She'd never worked with anyone quite as talented as him before and the sheer speed and skill of his fingers left her dragging behind. Fortunately her own natural ability asserted itself.

Don't think about him, she told herself firmly. *Think about the job*.

She kept her gaze fixed on those long, bronzed fingers, every nerve and muscle in her body tense as she focused on what he was doing.

Not once did he hesitate or pause. His fingers were precise and steady as he cleaned the skin, injected local anaesthetic and then aspirated the syringe to confirm the presence of blood.

It was no wonder he demanded the best from those around him, Liv thought as she handed him the scalpel and watched him incise the skin down to the rib with astonishing speed and precision. He was a master, and it was obvious that he wasn't satisfied with anything less than accuracy.

His handsome face blank of expression, he slid a gloved finger into the pleural cavity, checking the position of the incision. 'I'll want a 36F tube. Have it ready.'

'Roberts forceps.' Without being asked, Liv handed him the instrument she knew he'd need next and watched as he slid the drain into position through the track he'd made. Then he attached the tube to an underwater seal drainage system.

'That's a large tube he's used,' Phil muttered and Liv glanced at him briefly.

'It has to be of sufficient calibre to drain the haemothorax without clotting. And if the haemothorax doesn't drain, there's a risk of infection.' Her attention back on Stefano, she reached for the suture. 'Zero gauge suture.' She held it out to him and he took it immediately, their movements smooth and synchronised even though they'd never worked together in Resus before.

He inserted a purse-string suture to secure the drain and then glanced at the monitors again.

'I want another chest X-ray so that I can check the position of the drain.'

The radiographer hurried over and as they shifted the patient and took the X-ray, Phil glanced at the drain.

'He's losing a lot of blood. Should we clamp the tube?'

Stefano shook his head. 'Clamping the tube has no effect on the amount of haemorrhage—the blood just collects in the chest and further compromises respiratory function.'

'Mr Lucarelli? The X-ray is up on the screen,' the radiographer said and Liv glanced up as the door suddenly opened and Anna walked into the room.

'His wife's arrived. I've put her in the relatives' room,' she said. 'Can someone find a moment to talk to her?'

Liv glanced towards Stefano Lucarelli but the consultant was staring at the X-ray, his handsome face unsmiling and his concentration absolute. *He's young*, she thought, looking at his masculine profile and dark glossy hair. *Young to be in such a responsible position.* His strong legs were planted firmly apart, the thin cotton of the scrub suit skimming wide, muscular shoulders, his dark head tilted slightly as he studied the screen. He was staggeringly good-looking, confident and very much in control.

Realising that she was staring, Liv looked away quickly and caught Anna's speculative glance.

Her friend gave her a wide smile. 'I can see everything is going well in here.'

Liv glared at her. 'We'll talk to his wife in a minute, Anna.'

Stefano turned. 'We're waiting for the trauma surgeon.

When the patient is stable and they've decided on the next step, I'll talk to his wife.'

Phil studied the drain again. 'He's drained 1000 mils.'

'The initial volume of blood drained is not as important as ongoing bleeding.' Stefano looked up as the trauma surgeon strode into the room.

The two men conferred although Liv could see that the entire conversation was driven by Stefano Lucarelli.

Clearly his reputation was as formidable as his clinical skills because the senior trauma surgeon seemed only too happy to listen to his advice.

'I don't want to perform a thoracotomy unnecessarily.'

'I've used a large enough tube and it's positioned well.' Stefano glanced at the drain as if daring it to misbehave. 'It will drain the haemothorax. Admit him for observation, monitor the drainage output over the next four to five hours. If he loses more than 200 to 250 mils of blood per hour, take him to Theatre. I'm going to talk to his wife. Liv, come with me.'

Liv blinked. 'I— Yes, of course.'

She was about to make a mild comment about his dictatorial style when he looked at her, his gaze frank and direct. 'You're an excellent nurse. When I'm in Resus, I want you with me.'

'Oh…' The compliment was so unexpected that hot colour flooded her cheeks but she was saved the bother of replying because they'd reached the door of the relatives' room.

Without pausing, Stefano opened the door and strode into the room, leaving Liv to follow. She closed the door behind her, braced for him to open his mouth, put his foot in it and then walk out leaving the patient's relative distraught, a scenario she'd witnessed on all too many occasions with other doctors.

But instead of fumbling for words and making the quickest possible exit, he walked across to the patient's wife and sat down next to her. 'I am Stefano Lucarelli, the consultant. I've been looking after your husband.' He held out his hand and the woman shook it and gave a wobbly smile.

'I'm Helen Myers.'

'This has been a shock for you, I know.' He spoke in a deep, velvety voice that held equal amounts of confidence and sympathy. 'I am sorry I couldn't speak to you earlier, but your husband was my priority.'

'Of course—I understand.' The woman was white with shock, her eyes pink from crying. 'Is he—is he going to be all right?'

'He was kicked in the ribs and that kick has damaged his lung.' In simple, easy-to-understand terms, Stefano gave her the facts, explaining what had happened and the treatment he'd given so far. He kept it short and non-technical. 'Tim has been transferred to Intensive Care. They are going to monitor him and, if necessary, they will take him to Theatre and drain the blood clot.'

Tim? Liv blinked. She hadn't realised that he even knew the patient's name.

'Oh God, I can't believe this is happening. I saw him at lunch-time and we were making plans for Christmas. We were going to take our two girls to Lapland to see Santa Claus.' The woman sat still for a moment and then her face crumpled and she started to cry. 'I'm sorry, I'm really sorry, it's just that it's such a shock.'

Reaching for a box of tissues, Liv sat down on the other side of the woman and waited for Stefano to leave so that she could offer whatever comfort she could. But instead of leaving the room as fast as possible as most of his colleagues would have done, Stefano leaned across and took a tissue from the box.

'Don't apologise. It is hard for you, I know. Here.' He handed the woman the tissue. 'You mentioned that you have daughters? So who is looking after them now?'

'My mother.' Helen blew her nose hard. 'I called her as soon as I got the news. I didn't want to bring the children here. I'm sorry. You don't want to listen to this. I know how busy you must be. You have much more important things to do than talk to me.'

'At the moment, talking to you is the most important thing,' Stefano said calmly, his gaze not shifting from her face. 'Is there anything else you want to ask me?'

Helen gave a choked laugh. 'I want to ask you if he's going to be all right, but you can't tell me that, can you?'

'Not at this stage,' Stefano said honestly. 'The consultant in Intensive Care will be able to give you a better idea in a few hours.'

He was good, Liv thought to herself. Really, really good. He was honest, didn't give false hope and didn't try and escape from the emotions in front of him. And despite the workload pressing down on him, he seemed to really care.

'Liv will stay with you for a few minutes,' Stefano said, 'and then she will ring ICU.'

Liv gave an inward smile. *He was also controlling.* 'Once they have him settled, I'll take you up there,' she assured Helen and the woman blew her nose again.

'Thanks. You've been incredibly kind, both of you.' Tucking her handkerchief up her sleeve, she tried to smile. 'Men. Why must they play these dangerous sports?'

Stefano rose to his feet, a sardonic smile touching his mouth. 'We are incomprehensible, no? Blame it on testosterone.' Suddenly he sounded very Italian and Liv felt her insides tingle.

She found herself wondering if some glamorous, skinny woman was at that moment lying naked in his enormous bed, waiting for his return.

Horrified by the direction of her thoughts, she rose to her

feet. 'I'll make you a cup of tea, Helen,' she said quickly. 'And then I'll find out what's happening in ICU.' And while she was at it, she was going to bang her head against the wall a few times to try and reprogramme her thoughts back to the place they'd been before the conversation with Anna.

Why on earth was she envying a woman she hadn't even met for having something that she didn't even want?

She was definitely losing her grip.

CHAPTER TWO

'Mummy, can we have a *really* big Christmas tree this year? Up to the roof?'

'Absolutely.' Liv tried not to dwell on just how much 'really big' was going to cost. Maybe if she waited until Christmas Eve she could negotiate a bargain. 'How was school today?'

'Fine. I want to get our tree at the weekend.' Max scrambled onto a chair and spread his toy dinosaurs over the kitchen table. 'Then we can enjoy it for ages and ages.'

'It's only December the first. 'If we buy it on Saturday it will have no needles by Christmas.'

'If we don't buy our tree till Christmas Eve we won't have time to have fun with it. Sam is getting his tree next weekend. Can we? *Please?*' Max looked up at her hopefully and Liv felt something shift inside her.

'We'll see,' she said gruffly, promising herself that she'd sit down with a pen and paper once he was asleep and take a serious look at her budget. 'I love you. Have I told you that, lately?'

'Every day. You're always telling me that.'

'Are you complaining?'

'Nope.' Max picked up a plastic tyrannosaurus. 'I love you, too. It snowed again today, but not much. I want there to be piles and piles. Wouldn't that be great?'

Seeing the sparkle in her son's eyes, Liv forgot about the havoc that snow always caused. 'Fantastic.'

'Ben broke his leg yesterday.' Lower lip between his teeth, Max crashed the tyrannosaurus into a less superior species and sent it flying. 'He went to the hospital and they gave him crotches.'

Liv hid a smile. 'Crutches,' she said, spreading creamy butter onto crusty bread, 'it's crutches.'

'That's what I said. I told him my mum works in the hospital, but he said he didn't see you there. You won't work on Christmas Day, will you?'

Liv felt her heart flip. Every year she faced this dilemma. The money was good and in her situation that was incredibly tempting, but working Christmas meant not being with Max.

'I'm not working,' she said firmly, putting the plate on the table next to Max. It didn't matter how tight her finances were, nothing would make up for not spending Christmas Day with her son. 'I've saved up my holiday. I have a whole week off. I might work on New Year's Eve, but not until you're in bed.'

'So I'll do a sleepover with Sam?'

'Maybe. I'll have to speak to Anna.' Liv filled the kettle, wondering what she'd do if her friend and colleague hadn't had a child the same age as hers.

'Cool. I love sleeping over with Sam.' He looked at her, his eyes sparkling. 'Do you know what the best thing is about his house?'

No, but she could guess. Liv's heart plummeted as she thought of Sam's house, with its five large bedrooms, three bathrooms and huge garden. Then her eyes scanned the tiny living room of her cramped flat. If she stood in the middle, she could almost touch all four walls. And although she had two bedrooms, one of them was so small it would barely accommodate a single bed. And when the train went past the entire flat shook…

Aware that Max was looking at her, she braced herself. 'So what's the best thing about Sam's house?'

'Their guinea pig. It's called Rambo and it's *so* cute.'

Liv laughed and then impulsively she bent down and kissed her son, *the son who had noticed the guinea pig instead of the huge bedrooms or the soft white sofas and wall-to-wall luxury.*

'You're a nice person,' she said gruffly, but her eyes were drawn to the patch of damp on the wall. She'd painted over it repeatedly but it always came through again and now that the weather had turned cold…

Suddenly she wished she could wave a magic wand and make the world perfect for her son. Why was it that no one told you that parenthood came with non-stop guilt and anxiety? Especially *single* parenthood.

Telling herself that she was doing all right, Liv watched as her son played a make-believe game with his toys. He was bright, happy and well adjusted. She worried too much.

Everything was fine.

Max lifted his head and looked at her wistfully. 'And Sam's dad's buying him a goal for Christmas so he can practise. You should see it, Mum. It's just *awesome.* It's huge, with a big white net—I've seen the picture. Could we have a goal?'

'Not in a fourth-floor flat,' Liv said dryly, squashing down the guilt that swamped her once again. He was a little boy. He needed a garden. Somewhere he could kick a ball when she was too tired to take him to the park.

'If we had loads of money, would we buy a house? I heard you telling Anna that if you had a bathroom like hers, you'd lie in it all day. Why don't you lie in ours all day?'

Because of the chipped tiles, the draught from the window and the stubborn black mould that refused to die. 'Because I have to work. I've explained that to you. I work to make the money we need.' Liv lifted an onion out of the vegetable basket. 'Now, enough of this conversation. If I don't get on with the supper it will be bedtime.'

The tyrannosaurus attacked again, scattering other dinosaurs over the kitchen floor. 'You could do the lottery or something.'

'It's a waste of money. We wouldn't win.'

'You could get married. Emma's mum got married again and now they're really rich because her new dad is *loaded*!'

Liv gasped. 'Where did you hear that expression?'

'Emma told me.' Max stopped playing and looked at her anxiously. 'Is it swearing?'

'No, but it's not very polite.' Her mind slid back to the conversation she'd had with Anna earlier that day and she frowned, pushing away thoughts of Stefano Lucarelli. 'And it isn't how much money someone has that counts, it's whether you like them or not that matters.'

'Well, Emma's mum has been married twice now, and you've only been married once.'

'It isn't a competition, sweetheart.'

'Why did you stop being married?'

Liv closed her eyes briefly. Why did the hardest questions always come when she was tired? 'We've talked about this before, Max.' She peeled the onion. 'Sometimes these things just don't work out. And when that happens, it's no one's fault.' Yes it was. It was her fault. She hadn't been exciting enough for Jack. Her eyes suddenly started pricking and she told herself it was just the onion.

'You should definitely try being married again,' Max said

sagely. 'You're always telling me I have to keep trying things. You always say you can't tell if you like something if you've only tried it once.'

'That's food,' Liv said dryly, reaching for a chopping board. 'Marriage isn't like broccoli. Marriage is a very big thing. You have to really, really love someone to do that. And they have to love you, too. They have to think you're special.'

'You *are* special, Mum.' Max looked at her, his eyes huge. 'I don't know any other girls who love football and cars and *no one* makes pizza like you do. All my friends think you're cool.'

'Well, maybe I am cool to a bunch of seven-year-olds.' But bigger boys wanted something very different. They wanted someone sexy and she was—

Ordinary.

Liv stood for a moment, distracted by her own thoughts. Across the road she could see lights from the other flats and in one window she could see a man and a woman sitting down to eat with two lively, excited children.

Then she glanced at Max. Her little boy, his face a mask of concentration as he lined up his dinosaurs. She paused for a moment, swamped by a feeling of such intense love and anxiety that she almost couldn't breathe.

He deserved so much more. He deserved a loving father who would kick a football with him.

Damn Jack. Damn Jack and his slick, womanising ways.

She put the onion on the chopping board and stabbed the knife through it.

Why should Max suffer because his father hadn't been adult enough to face up to his responsibilities?

'Mummy, you're chopping that onion like you *hate* it or something.'

Liv's gaze slid from the blade in her hand to the minute

slices of onion that now lay on the chopping board. Pulverised. She gave a weak smile. 'I'm making supper.' *There was no point in regretting the past.* 'We can play football together this weekend, if you like.'

'Cool. I've been picked for the match on Friday. I was a reserve but now Ben can't play so I'm in the team.'

Liv's face lit up. 'That's fantastic! Why didn't you tell me before?'

'It's only the second team, not the first.' He looked at her and his little shoulders lifted in a tiny shrug. 'And I knew you wouldn't be able to come. You'll be working.'

Liv swallowed. 'Max—'

'It's OK,' he said firmly. 'It isn't your fault. We're a team, isn't that what you always say? You go to work, I go to school.'

'Actually I'm not working on Friday,' Liv said brightly. 'I—I have the afternoon off.'

'Really?'

No. 'Yes.' Somehow, whatever it took, she was going to make it happen. She was going to her son's football match. 'What time is kick-off?'

'Two o'clock.'

'I'll be there.' How, she didn't know. But she was going to be standing on that school field even if it meant changing her job.

Exhaustion washed over her making her head foggy. As usual her day had started before five and one glance at the washing, ironing and the pile of Max's toys in the living room was enough to tell her that she wouldn't be in bed before midnight.

She envied mothers who could be at home for their children. Yes, she loved her work but the constant pressure of trying to be in two places at once was grinding her down.

Welcome to single parenthood.

Max scrambled off the chair and hugged her tightly, his arms round her legs, his head pressed against her stomach. 'You're the best mum in the world. I know it's hard for you because you have to work. That would be one of the good things about having a dad. He could do the work bit and you could just come and watch me.'

Liv felt a lump in her throat. 'There's more to being a dad than signing cheques, Max.' *And some men didn't even manage that bit*, she thought wearily as she bent to kiss the top of his head. He smelled of shampoo. 'Spaghetti bolognese all right for supper?'

'Yum.'

Dismissing fantasies of herself standing on the school field, while someone else worried about the family finances, Liv squashed down the guilt, gave him a quick kiss and released him. *Reality*, she reminded herself. That was what she had to concentrate on. 'So what was the funniest thing that happened to you today?' Taking the lid off a can of tomatoes, she emptied it into the pan. 'Make me laugh.'

'Sam told me a great joke.'

'Go on.'

'What's the best thing to give a seasick elephant?'

'I don't know. What is the best thing to give a seasick elephant?'

'Plenty of room.'

'Max!'

The following morning brought a flutter of snow and a sharp drop in the temperature.

'Isabella? *Tutto bene?*' Stefano brought the Ferrari to a smooth halt, his attention on the phone call. Snow dusted the pavements and the roads were slick with ice. It was going to be a busy day in the emergency department and he knew this would be his only chance to make this call. 'You called me?'

'Every day for the past two weeks!' His sister exploded into Italian. 'Where have you been? You don't call—you don't come home! Have you forgotten your family? Don't we matter to you any more? *You don't have a heart, Stefano!*'

'That's the sort of comment I expect from my girlfriend, not my little sister.' Stefano sprang from the car, his long, black, cashmere coat swirling around his strong legs as he strode across the consultants' car park. Knowing *exactly* which buttons to press to annoy her, he smiled wickedly. 'Why are you at home? You should be taking your children to school.'

Ever predictable, Isabella bristled with indignation. 'I dropped them at school and now I'm on the way to the office. Remember the family business, Stefano? The business you turned your back on? Well I am here, keeping our father happy while you stroke your ego by playing doctors and dating actresses with bodies as thin as spaghetti and brains as soft as ravioli.'

Already bored with the conversation, Stefano pushed his way through the swing doors that led to the emergency department. 'Are you ringing me to nag me about my choice of career or my choice of women?'

'I'm ringing you because despite your many faults, you're still my brother and like all men you need reminding about family responsibility. When did you last call Papa?'

Stefano strode along the corridor, oblivious to the sideways glances he received from the female nurses. 'I don't have any news.'

'News? What is "news"?' Isabella didn't bother hiding her exasperation. 'He just wants to hear your voice, Stefano!'

'Talking about nothing because you enjoy the sound of your own voice is more of a girl thing than a man thing,' Stefano drawled. 'And I've been busy. I'm working.'

'Well, find the time to call. And make sure you come home for Christmas. We'll all be in Cortina from the twenty-third of December.'

Stefano was well able to picture the scene: a noisy group of family and old friends descending on the enormous family chalet in the exclusive mountain resort of Cortina D'Ampezzo, in the Italian Dolomites.

'Isabella—'

'I know you're busy, but this is family time, Stefano. Be there.'

'I will be there, but I don't know when or for how long.' *Or how much of his well-meaning, interfering family he'd be able to stand.*

'All the cousins will be there—' it was Isabella's turn to tease '—including the lovely Donatella. She's still single, Stefano.'

'Fortunately for both of us, my taste in women doesn't run to children,' Stefano said wryly and Isabella giggled.

'She's twenty-one, Stefano, hardly a child. And she's been trying to remind you of that fact for a few years now. Surely you haven't forgotten last Christmas? The push-up bra and the low-cut top? I thought Papa was going to have a stroke. Anyway, she wants to sit by you for Christmas Eve dinner.'

'Donatella finds me so intimidating that she can barely speak in my company,' Stefano reminded her in an acid tone. 'If you throw her in my way at Christmas it would be cruel to both of us. Isabella, drop this subject.'

'She'd be a traditional Italian wife, Stefano.' Isabella was clearly enjoying herself. 'She would stay at home and cook you pasta.'

'Unfortunately for Donatella one of my requirements in a life partner is that they're able to sustain an intelligent conversation for at least eight seconds. Sadly, she can't. Or at least, she can't when she's with me.'

Isabella snorted with laughter. 'You're so harsh. Frankly I can't see why she's so crazy about you. I mean, I know you're filthy rich and good-looking but you're *unbearable* to people who aren't as bright as you are and when you're *really* bored, which usually takes far less than eight seconds by the way, you can be horribly cutting.'

Taken aback by that blunt assessment of his attributes, Stefano was about to answer when his sister made an impatient sound.

'Anyway, it's nonsense to say you need a woman with a brain. According to that actress of yours, you don't waste any time talking to women.'

Stefano glanced at his watch. 'I'm a busy man, Isabella. Was there something else you wanted to say?'

'She gave *such* an embarrassing interview to all the papers. What did you ever see in her? No—don't answer that, it's obvious. *Why* are men so shallow?'

Stefano gave a deadly smile. 'Because women wear push-up bras and we are easily distracted,' he purred. 'I'm so pleased you called me. Your conversation is always so…intellectual.'

'Don't try and intimidate me.' But Isabella was laughing. 'I rang you for a chat because I love you, even though you sometimes forget that you have a family and you're basically horrible. I'll see you at Christmas, Stefano. I'm sure Donatella is already choosing her dress.'

Stefano closed his eyes briefly. '*Maledizione*—'

'Don't swear in front of your sister!'

There was a sharp rap on the door and Stefano looked up

with a frown, irritated by the interruption. Greg Hampton, one of the casualty officers, stood in the doorway and Stefano's mouth tightened. Unlike Phil who had managed to impress him, this particular junior doctor's attitude was far too casual for his liking. 'I've got to go. *Ciao.*' He terminated the call and dropped his phone into his pocket. '*Sì?* There is a problem?'

'Can you check an X-ray for me before you get dragged into Resus? Everyone else is still tied up with the RTA that came in an hour ago.'

Stefano slung his coat over the back of the chair, ignored the mound of paperwork on his desk and strode towards the door. 'Who is the patient?'

'That's the bad news.' Greg pulled a face. 'A screaming, un-cooperative kid with a bruised finger. I sent her for an X-ray.'

Stefano dealt him a measuring glance, less than impressed by the younger doctor's dismissive tone.

They arrived at the main area and Stefano automatically glanced at the computer screen on the wall. It listed every patient in the department and enabled the staff to track their progress. That one glance was enough to tell him that he was in for a busy morning despite the fact it was barely light.

His mind still half on the conversation with his sister, his gaze shifted to the smaller computer next to the screen that was displaying an X-ray of a finger. He hit a button, zoomed in closer and stared at the image. *Why did his family see the need to interfere with his life?* If it wasn't his love life, it was his profession. 'No fracture. How was the finger on examination?'

Greg shrugged. 'I haven't examined her yet.'

'You sent her for X-ray without examination?' Stefano transferred his gaze from the X-ray to the doctor and Greg frowned slightly.

'The child was really difficult. Didn't seem to want to be

distracted by anything. Trust me—no one could have done anything with this kid, and as for the mother…' with an exaggerated shudder, he picked up the notes '…she was your average nightmare. Reminded me why I didn't do paediatrics. Caring for kids is all about the mothers, isn't it? What's the point of seven years' training if I have to waste my skills on a load of hysterical women?'

'What skills?' Stefano spoke softly and Greg's smile lost a fraction of its arrogance.

'What do you mean?'

'You told me that you don't want to waste your skills,' Stefano said silkily, 'but I am still waiting to see a demonstration of these skills in which you have so much pride and which you seem so reluctant to waste in my department, Dr Hampton. They weren't in evidence when you needed to examine the child.'

Greg cleared his throat. 'I didn't manage to examine the child.'

'Precisely.' Stefano watched with cold detachment as the less experienced doctor flushed to the roots of his hair, suddenly a great deal less sure of himself.

'The kid was freaking out.'

'Then it is your job to "un"-freak them,' Stefano advised helpfully. 'After all, what is the point of seven years of training if you cannot get close enough to your patient to carry out an examination?'

'I ordered an X-ray,' Greg said stiffly, and Stefano raised an eyebrow.

'So you sent her to X-Ray with no examination and you were planning to discharge her without examination? You have good medical defence insurance, I hope? A skilled lawyer? Because if that is the way you practise medicine, you will need both.'

Greg's face was scarlet. 'I assumed that the X-ray would tell me what I needed to know.'

'An X-ray is simply one part of the overall picture. Never again even consider discharging a patient without carrying out the appropriate examination. You are a doctor, not a car mechanic. The decisions you make affect people's lives.' Stefano let the doctor squirm for a few more moments and then he flicked off the X-ray.

'Mr Lucarelli—'

'One more thing.' Stefano's icy tone cut through the doctor's feeble attempt to redeem himself. 'In this department, if a mother tells you that she has a bad feeling about her child, you will listen to what she has to say with both ears open and your mouth closed. Understood?'

Greg stared at him. 'Yes.'

'Good.' Stefano watched him with cool appraisal. 'Most mothers are uncannily accurate when it comes to assessing the health of their children. Remember that. They sense things that we doctors, even with years of training, can take longer to detect. Now, given that you have been unable to examine the patient, show me where she is and I will do it for you.'

Stiff and defensive, the casualty officer led the way down the corridor and into one of the small cubicles.

Prepared to deal with a very distressed child, Stefano stopped dead in the doorway, astonished to see the little girl laughing and smiling.

Liv was kneeling on the floor, chatting away happily and the child sat listening, clearly absorbed by the conversation. Her eyes were fixed on the nurse in fascination and Stefano found himself reacting in much the same way.

From his vantage point in the doorway, his gaze was drawn to the curve of her soft mouth and suddenly he found himself comparing the sweetness of her smile to Francine's sexy scarlet pout.

Surprised by the direction of his thoughts, Stefano wondered why he was comparing two women who were so blatantly unalike.

Francine was an actress and a model—her looks were part of her job. Whereas Liv—well, she was entirely different. She wasn't beautiful in the conventional sense. Her mouth was too wide and she had a pronounced dimple in her left cheek when she smiled, but there was something about her face that made it difficult to look away. Her eyes were bright and intelligent, and she radiated warmth and good humour as she talked to the child.

Stefano's gaze swept her body in an instinctive male appraisal.

Her uniform wasn't tight, but there was no missing her enticing curves and he felt the immediate and powerful response of his body. As irritated by his reaction as he was surprised, he turned his attention back to the child, assuming that it was just that ridiculous conversation with his sister that was suddenly turning his thoughts to sex in the middle of his working day.

'So you sit next to Annabel.' Liv spoke in a calm, gentle voice that removed all the stress from the room and smoothed Stefano's frayed nerves like the stroke of a velvet glove. 'And who is your teacher?'

'Miss Grant.' The little girl smiled at her. 'She has her hair in a ponytail, like you.'

'Well, that's the best way to wear it for work, especially if it's curly because it can get in your eyes. So how did you fall on your finger?'

Aware that Greg Hampton was about to speak, Stefano

silenced him with a lift of his hand and a searing glance, intensely irritated that the man would even *consider* intervening when the nurse clearly had full control of the situation.

Fortunately the child hadn't even noticed their presence. 'I did it yesterday. We were practising the nativity play,' she was saying, 'and I tripped over a sheep. I mean, not a real sheep, actually it was Gareth, dressed as a sheep. But I fell on my finger, I mean like *all* my weight was on my finger.'

Stefano watched as Liv listened attentively to the child's story and then carefully examined the child's finger.

Her hair was the rich brown of a conker and it gleamed and shone under the harsh emergency room lights. Although it had been pulled back into a ponytail, several curls had escaped and now drifted around her face. Having not looked twice at a woman for months, Stefano found himself staring. She wasn't wearing a trace of make-up and yet her lashes were thick and dark and her cheeks had a healthy glow. But what really drew his attention was her absolute focus on the little girl.

She wasn't thinking about herself or her appearance. She hadn't even noticed that he was standing in the doorway.

Suddenly his mind drifted back to the conversation he'd overheard the day before.

Why did Anna want to buy her hot sex for Christmas?

Stefano dismissed the question instantly as one of those things that women laugh about and men are better off not knowing.

But his eyes trailed back to her mouth and lower.

She didn't look like a woman who needed someone else to find her hot sex.

Why had Anna been hugging her? Had something happened? Was there something wrong in her life?

'Ouch. That's the bit that really hurts.' The little girl winced as Liv gently manipulated her fingers.

'It's bound to hurt because it's really bruised, can you see? It's just a bit black there—over the joint. I think you're incredibly brave.'

The little girl looked doubtful. 'I *was* crying.'

'I'm not surprised.' Liv's tone suggested that anything less would have been unthinkable. 'If it were my finger, I would have cried, too. I think you've been amazing. But what we need to do now is fix it so that it doesn't hurt so much. What were you in the nativity play?'

'A star. Is it broken?'

'Well, I'm going to take a look at your X-ray and then have a chat with the doctor.'

'Not the same doctor as before?' The child shrank slightly. 'He was really angry with me—' Suddenly noticing Greg in the doorway, she snatched her hand back. *'He's not going to touch me.'*

The atmosphere altered in the blink of an eye.

Deciding that swift intervention was called for if he wasn't to lose all chances of examining the child himself, Stefano cast a meaningful glance towards his less experienced colleague and strolled into the room.

'Ciao, cucciola mia.' He addressed the little girl directly but her eyes were fixed on Greg in horror.

'I don't want him to be my doctor.'

'He isn't your doctor.'

'So why is he here?'

'Because he works with me.' Well aware that his height and physique could make him intimidating, Stefano dropped into a crouch so that he was at the same level as the child. 'So you fell off a stage, is that right?'

'Yes.' Finally the little girl looked at him and her expression was curious. 'Why do you speak with a funny accent?'

Stefano smiled. 'Because I'm from Italy.'

'Like pizza? I love pizza.'

'Just like pizza. So tell me…' Stefano gently took her hand in his and examined her fingers '…what is your favourite pizza?'

'Margarita, but not too cheesy and no lumps of tomatoes.'

'Obviously you are a woman who knows what she wants.' Amused, Stefano turned the child's hand over. 'Show me how you fell on your hand.'

'I fell all on one finger, like this…' The little girl pretended to stab the ground and Stefano pulled a face.

'Well, that is why your finger is hurting. You are supposed to walk on your feet, not your finger.' Gently he manipulated the finger. 'Does this hurt? This? Can you squeeze—make a fist?'

As he examined the dark bruising over the back of the finger, he was acutely conscious of Liv next to him. He allowed himself one sideways glance, but she wasn't even looking at him. All her attention was still focused on her little patient.

'I thought it was probably a volar plate injury,' she murmured and Stefano silently compared her calm efficiency with Greg's ineffectual arrogance.

'I agree.' Impressed, he gave her a rare smile but she didn't even seem to notice.

She didn't blush, stare or send him a subtly flirtatious look. In fact she didn't look at him at all. Instead, she rose to her feet, her eyes still on the little girl. 'You'll have to be careful with that finger for a few weeks, Bella.'

Stefano was so accustomed to being cautious in his interaction with women that for a moment he was taken aback by her apparent indifference to him.

For a brief moment in Resus yesterday he'd felt a powerful explosion of chemistry and he was sure that she'd felt it too. But clearly it had been his imagination.

He almost laughed at himself. Had he really grown so arrogant that he expected every woman to look at him?

Unfortunately the child's mother *was* looking at him with what she obviously believed to be feminine allure.

'You're the consultant?' She scanned Stefano's face and her eyes widened slightly. 'What's a volar plate? I've never heard of it.'

Stefano ignored the look in her eyes and kept his response cool and professional. 'Your finger joints are like a hinge, yes? They must bend and straighten. The bones are connected together by tough bands of tissue called ligaments. In this joint— we call it the PIP—the strongest ligament is the volar plate.'

The mother studied his face a little more intently than was necessary. 'So she's pulled a ligament? Like a sprain, you mean?'

Instinctively adjusting his body language to create distance, Stefano stepped back. 'This particular ligament connects the proximal phalanx to the middle phalanx on the palm side of the joint.'

'These two joints,' Liv said quickly, demonstrating on her own hand and Stefano gave a faint smile because he realised that he'd made his explanation far too complicated, which was unlike him.

But he'd been extricating himself from the flirtatious glances of the mother.

Forcing his mind back onto his work, he tried again. 'The ligament tightens as the joint is straightened and keeps the joint from hyper-extending—bending too far back, in other words. But if you do overextend this joint, the volar plate can be damaged.'

The little girl's face drooped with disappointment. 'So does that mean I can't be a star in the nativity?'

Unusually for him, Stefano found himself at a loss. 'What exactly does a star do?'

'I dance a bit and then I stand still while the shepherds walk towards me.'

'That will be fine,' Stefano assured her. 'Just be careful not to fall over any more sheep.'

'Is it broken?'

'Not exactly broken, just damaged. And we're going to have to give it some help to make it better.'

'Will I have a plaster that everyone in my class can sign?'

'No. We're going to give it a buddy to hold onto. This finger next to it—it will support your bad finger until it is healed. Your good finger will help your injured finger. Like a friend.' Stefano glanced at Liv. 'Can you arrange that for me?'

'Of course. And I expect you want her to go back to the hand clinic in ten days, to check that Bella has full movement in that finger.' She scribbled on a form and signed it. 'Now, if you just wait there, I'll strap that finger for you.'

'I know who you are.' The little girl's eyes narrowed. 'You're Max's mum, aren't you? You're called Liv.'

In the process of writing the notes, Stefano's hand stilled. *She had a child?*

He didn't know which surprised him most, the fact that she was some child's mother when she really didn't look old enough, or his own thunderous disappointment that she belonged to another man.

If she was married, why had Anna been offering to buy her hot sex for Christmas?

Seriously concerned by the alarming direction of his own thoughts, he scrawled in the notes and strode to the door. 'If you need anything else, call me,' he said in a cool tone but Liv didn't appear any more disconcerted by the chill than she'd been impressed by the smile. Instead she simply concentrated on applying Elastoplast strapping to the child's finger.

As they walked out of the door, Greg cleared his throat. 'Is everything all right, Mr Lucarelli?'

'That nurse is obviously very experienced,' Stefano said smoothly. 'My advice is to watch and learn. Next time you run into trouble with a child, ask for her help.'

Why did he care whether she was married?

What difference did it make to him?

He glanced over his shoulder just as Liv lifted her left hand to remove a piece of strapping. And Stefano noticed one more thing about her.

Her finger was bare. She wasn't wearing a wedding ring.

CHAPTER THREE

HER heart thudding frantically in her chest, Liv finished strapping Bella's finger and gave the mother a set of instructions.

It had proved really, really hard to work shoulder to shoulder with Stefano Lucarelli without once looking at him, but somehow she'd managed it.

Not that her display of willpower had done anything to reduce the effect he had on her. Whenever he was in the room, her body felt oddly lethargic, her skin tingled and there was a tiny thrill in her stomach that took her breath away.

Chemistry.

No, not chemistry. That implied something shared and there was no way he would feel the same way about her. Which meant that what she was feeling was...lust. Good old-fashioned lust.

Well, whatever it was called it was extremely irritating and inconvenient, she thought to herself crossly, as she directed mother and child back towards the exit. It had been the same the previous day in Resus. One glance was all it had taken. The look itself had probably lasted for less than a second, but the aftershocks had been with her all day and the depth of her reaction shocked her because she'd had no idea she was even *capable* of experiencing that sudden fiery burn of sexual awareness.

It was all Anna's fault. If they hadn't had that ridiculous conversation about sex, Liv wouldn't have noticed Stefano Lucarelli.

Or maybe she would.

With an exasperated sigh, Liv dried her hands and forced herself to think about Jack, something she usually avoided at all costs. But desperate times called for desperate measures. *If she thought about Jack, she'd remember why she was single.*

Having thoroughly depressed herself, she was just about to call her next patient when Anna slid into the room, her eyes gleaming wickedly.

'You'll never guess what.'

Liv slipped her scissors back into her pocket. 'No, I probably wouldn't but I'm glad you're here, because I need to ask a favour.'

'Anything.' Anna waved her hand airily. 'Since our irascible consultant has taken a shine to you, you're my best asset. But if it's a pay rise, forget it.'

'Can I work a split shift on Friday? Max has been picked for the football team.'

'Really?' Anna's face brightened. 'That's fantastic. Yes, work a split. I'll juggle the rota if I have to. Why don't you let me pick him up from school afterwards and he can do a sleepover with Sam.'

'I can't ask you to do that—'

'You'd be doing me a favour. If the boys are playing, I can write my Christmas cards. They've been glaring at me from inside their packaging for the past two weeks.'

Liv smiled. 'All right. Thanks so much.' It would save her having to beg yet another favour, this time from the childminder.

'It's the least I can do for Super-Nurse. Our cool, hard-to-please consultant is sending shivers of terror throughout the department but apparently *you* make the grade.' Anna's smile was wicked. 'He strode up to me this morning and said in his most commanding voice, *"When I am in Resus, I want Leev with me."* The way he says your name is incredibly sexy.'

Liv tried to ignore the bump of her heart. 'You need to work on your Italian accent. That was a terrible imitation.'

'What exactly did you do to him in Resus to make him love you so much? I really want to know. I'm trying not to be offended by the fact he clearly thinks the rest of us are rubbish.'

'We just worked well together.'

Anna gave a slow smile. 'Obviously you make a lovely couple. Have you invited him to the Snowflake Ball yet?'

'No, I haven't invited him to the Snowflake Ball, because I'm not going.'

'You should invite him. At least then you'll have something to tell your grandchildren.' Anna glanced over her shoulder to check they were alone and then whipped a piece of paper out of her pocket. 'One of the nurses in fracture clinic looked Sexy Stefano up on the internet and came across an interview with his ex—some gorgeous blonde Italian actress.' She unfolded the paper. 'Listen to this—*"One of the drawbacks of Italian men is that they're extremely macho and dominating."*' Anna glanced up. 'Is that a drawback? I'd give anything for David to ignore the fact that I'm loading the dishwasher and just throw me down onto the sofa for a bit of wild sex.'

'Anna, for goodness' sake—'

'You haven't heard anything yet.' Anna cleared her throat. '*"Stefano was so hot tempered and passionate that our entire relationship sometimes felt like one long blazing series of rows and reconciliation."*'

Unsettled by the conversation, Liv concentrated on putting the dressings away. 'That doesn't sound very relaxing. I'm not surprised they broke up.'

'Hold on, I'm just coming to the best bit—"*Maybe it's because he's a doctor, but he knew exactly what to do to my body. He was so skilled in bed and so demanding that for six months I was too tired to get up in the morning. My career almost fell apart. Two words come to mind when I think of Stefano and they are sex and stamina.*" All right, now I'm jealous.' Anna scrunched the paper up and threw it in the bin in disgust. 'I can't remember the last time I was kept awake by a man's ravenous libido.'

'This is too much information.' Liv covered her ears. 'I really like your husband.'

'I like him too, and it's as much my fault as his. Life is so exhausting that when I see my bed I just want to sleep in it, not set fire to the sheets. I wish I hadn't read that article. I was relatively happy with my life until I realised that I could be having hot sex all night with a luscious trauma surgeon who knows exactly what to do with my body. I mean, can you imagine waking up in the morning next to Stefano Lucarelli?'

'No, I can't imagine it because it would be too terrible for words.' Liv shuddered. 'It would be daylight and I would never have the confidence to show my body to anyone in daylight. He'd probably be sick.'

Anna gaped at her. 'You have absolutely no idea how lovely you are.'

'Oh yes.' Liv gave a mocking a smile. 'So lovely that Jack could barely drag himself away from me to sleep with other women.'

'Jack was just a—' Anna used a word that made Liv blink.

'I can't believe you just said that. Wash your mouth out.'

'I just hate the way he's made you feel about your-self,' Anna said simply. 'Because of him, you have no self-confidence. Just do me a favour—try smouldering at Stefano and see what happens.'

'He'd probably throw a bucket of water over me and I wouldn't blame him.'

'He's seriously rich, gorgeous and single. If you're not even prepared to flirt with him then you need therapy,' Anna said and Liv smiled.

'Anna, darling, one of us definitely needs therapy, but I don't think it's me.'

'Are you telling me that you can look him in the eye and not think of sex?'

'Stop talking about sex!' The words came out louder than she'd intended and Liv slammed a hand over her mouth and giggled in disbelief. 'For crying out loud, Anna, what is the matter with you? Go to lunch, or go and have a cold shower or—something.'

'"Or something" sounds good but unfortunately I'll have to settle for lunch.' Anna handed her the keys to the drug cupboard. 'You're in charge. Hire and fire at will. Try not to get up to anything while I'm gone.' She walked briskly out of the room and Liv pinned the keys in her pocket with hands that weren't quite steady.

All this talk of sex was starting to unsettle her.

Her eyes slid to the article in the bin.

Did he know what to do with his hands? Well, of course he did. He was a good-looking, confident, experienced man. He didn't fumble in Resus and she didn't for a moment expect him to fumble in the bedroom. He just wasn't that type of guy.

She gave a sigh of exasperation. Pretending that she hadn't noticed him or that he wasn't attractive was just silly. Who was she kidding? Everyone had noticed him and with good reason.

Wealthy, good-looking doctors weren't exactly a common species. Most of the doctors she worked with were pale-skinned and out of shape, like plants that had been deprived of sunlight. Stefano's bronzed skin and Mediterranean good looks made him stand out like a bold sunflower in a field of withered dandelions.

But what really stayed in her mind was his skill as a doctor. He was breathtakingly skilled and ruthless in his demands for perfection, and yet at the same time he'd shown himself capable of displaying a surprising degree of compassion when it was required. He was gorgeous.

Seriously worried by her own thoughts, she gave herself a sharp talking to. *Enough!* Even *thinking* of him in that way was embarrassing. He was smooth, sophisticated and stunning whereas she was—she was…

Delusional, Liv thought, exasperated with herself. Delusional, for thinking that a man like him might be interested in someone like her.

Ordinary, wasn't that what Jack had called her?

Ordinary. Dependable.

She was a good nurse, a loving mother and a caring friend. But she wasn't sexy or glamorous.

And she wasn't the sort of woman that a man like Stefano Lucarelli would ever notice.

She needed to stop thinking about sex and get on with her life.

'Down the wing, Max, *down the wing*!'

Two days later Liv stood on edge of the school field with a row of parents. Several of the men had obviously taken the afternoon off from work to cheer the children on in their football match.

And it was cold. Really cold. Liv had wrapped a scarf

around her neck but her breath clouded the freezing air and her fingers were numb.

'Hi, Liv. You've met my husband, Simon, haven't you?' The mother of a boy in Max's class was standing huddled next to a stocky, cheerful-looking man whose polished shoes looked out of place on the school playing field. A toddler slept in a pushchair next to her and every now and then she jiggled the handle to keep him asleep. Even under the large winter coat, it was obvious that she was very pregnant.

'Hi, Simon.' Liv smiled. 'How are you, Claire? When's the baby due?'

'Christmas Day.' Claire cast a teasing glance towards her husband. 'You'll be cooking the turkey, sunshine. Better start practising.'

'Ah—I had something to tell you about that.' Simon was concentrating hard on the game, his eyes following the ball. 'I've invited my mother to stay at Christmas. It seemed like a good idea. *Go on, James!*'

'You've invited your mother? Are you kidding?!' Claire's mouth dropped open but Simon was urging the team on and didn't respond. Claire glanced at Liv and rolled her eyes. 'Men! At the first hint of domestic work, they ring their mothers.'

Simon dragged his eyes from the pitch for half a second. 'Did you really want to eat my turkey?'

Claire glared at him. 'So you're going to be on the sofa watching the TV?'

His eyes were back on the pitch. 'I do my bit.'

'Oh, really?'

'Yes, really! I'm the one that's been coaching James on his football skills. And just look at him go!' Simon gazed at his son proudly and Liv felt something uncurl inside her. *Something uncomfortable that made her feel slightly sick.*

She looked away quickly, reminding herself that she could kick a football with her son, too. *But it wasn't the same, was it?* Sometimes she just ached when she saw the way Max stared longingly at the fathers playing with their sons in the park. She'd seen the way he sidled up to the fringes of other male groups, hoping to be included.

The truth was that there was no male influence in his life and he needed one. If she had the money she would have given him football coaching for his Christmas present but that was out of the question.

She was his football coach. She was everything.

Liv turned her attention back to the football match, shocked by the thick sludge of jealousy that surged through her veins.

Hating herself for feeling that way, she gritted her teeth. It wasn't like her. She was incredibly lucky. She had a son she adored and a job she loved—a good life.

Her eyes slid back towards Claire and Simon who were still sharing a laugh together at the prospect of their crazy, noisy Christmas.

But she didn't have anyone to share her life with, did she?

Perhaps Anna was right. Perhaps it was time she thought about dating again. But she really didn't think she had the courage. Perhaps if she used the internet and said *SINGLE MOTHER WITH CHILD*, at least that would warn people that she wasn't a supermodel. But she had to put something nice about herself. *Can make pizza, kick a football and read bedtime stories?* What sort of person would that attract?

The truth was that the mere thought of internet dating, horrified her. What if someone met her in the flesh and thought, Yuck?

Shrinking at the thought, Liv concentrated on the game. She watched as Max sped down the field, a determined look on his face as he chased the ball. His little legs were bruised and muddy and his football shirt was so long it looked as though he wasn't wearing any shorts, but he was trying so hard that he was almost bursting. *He looked so small and vulnerable*, Liv thought to herself, wondering whether parenthood affected everyone like this.

When she looked at him she just ached, wanting everything to be all right for him.

Dating when she was single had been hard enough. Dating with a child didn't bear thinking about. This time it wasn't just her who would be hurt when it all went wrong.

Conscious of Claire's husband yelling at his son, she wrapped her arms around herself and tried to subdue the envy. There *were* men out there prepared to shoulder the responsibility of family. It was just that she hadn't found one. Maybe she would, one day. Someone who wouldn't think Yuck when he saw her. Someone who would see past the fact that she wasn't sexy and value her other qualities.

She watched as Max's foot made contact with the ball and it flew into the goal. Max yelled triumphantly and all his teammates jumped on him, barely able to contain their excitement.

Liv clapped her hands and Claire and Simon gave a little whoop.

'Did you see me, Mum?' He came running over; her little boy with shining eyes and cheeks pink from the cold. 'Did you see me?'

'I saw you.' She bent and hugged him, loving the fact that he still wanted her to do that, despite the presence of his friends. 'You were brilliant.'

'I love football, Mum. I love it.'

'I know you do.' Liv hugged him tightly, breathing in the smell of little boy and muddy field.

'Are you going to work now?'

'Yes. And you're going home with Anna and Sam. Be good. I'll pick you up tomorrow morning.'

'Great, bye Mum.' He turned and sped across the field to join his friends who were making their way back towards the school.

Swallowing down the lump in her throat, Liv said a quick goodbye to Claire and Simon and walked towards her car. Having taken a few hours off in the middle of the day, she was due back at the hospital. No time to mope or feel sorry for herself. The reality of her life. Work. If she didn't work, there was no money.

The moment she walked through the doors, Stefano Lucarelli strode up to her. '*Where* have you been?' His raw masculinity took her breath away and Liv felt the instantaneous reaction of her body. Her heart pounded, her knees weakened and she felt horribly light-headed. To make matters worse, the interview with the actress was fresh in her mind and suddenly she had a disturbingly vivid image of him sliding those strong, confident hands over the pliant shivering body of a sickeningly slender woman.

Flustered, she unwrapped the scarf from around her neck. 'I had a few hours off this afternoon.'

'In the middle of your shift?' He stood in front of her, legs spread in a confrontational stance, blocking her path. For a moment she couldn't speak. Sexual awareness burned hot and dangerous and every thought was blown from her head except one. *He'd noticed that she hadn't been working.* For a reason that she didn't want to examine, she felt like singing and dancing, but somehow she managed to keep her feet still.

'You were looking for me?'

Maybe the feelings weren't all on her side.

'*Sì*, I was looking for you. We had a very distressed child with a fractured tibia,' he growled. '*I needed you.*'

A distressed child.

Liv returned to reality with such a bump that every part of her felt bruised even though she hadn't moved a muscle. Disappointment swamped her like a flutter of freezing snow. He'd needed her. *At work.* Of course, at work. 'There are other nurses.'

'I was given other nurses. And they were slow. I had to *ask* for the instruments I needed,' he said scathingly, 'and they had *no* idea how to comfort the child. *Where were you?*'

Liv didn't know whether to laugh or cry.

She should be grateful to him, she told herself. It was just the wake-up call she needed. She wasn't the sort of woman a man turned to when he needed hot sex, she was the sort of woman a man turned to when he needed something done. 'I'm working a split shift, today. I went to watch my son play football.'

The thunderous expression on his face vanished and his mouth curved into an unexpected smile. 'He plays football? Did he score?'

Transfixed by that smile and the sudden change in him, Liv blinked. 'Y-yes, actually,' she stammered finally. 'He did. He was thrilled.' *And he wanted to be picked for the first team but she had no idea how to coach him properly.*

His eyes lingered on her face for a long, unsettling moment. 'So why are you looking so worried?'

'Worried?' She was so astonished that he'd noticed that the word came out like a squeak and she almost laughed at herself. *Talk about unsophisticated.* Anna would have thought of something flirtatious and clever to say, but she couldn't even hold a conversation with the man without her tongue tying itself into a knot. 'I'm not worried.'

'But something is wrong.' His eyes didn't shift from her face. 'Tell me.'

She stared up into the dark glitter of his eyes and felt her stomach flip. Oh boy. *My son needs a father, I need a make-over, I'm broke and it's Christmas in three weeks.*

Liv gave a laugh, trying to imagine his face if she spilled out her problems. 'Nothing is wrong. I'd better go.' Before her thoughts and her words became mixed up. 'I'll be back in the department in a minute, Mr Lucarelli.'

And by then she would have pulled herself together.

She needed to stop dreaming, before she embarrassed herself. *What was the matter with her?* Normally, she was realistic and practical. Even if she were single with no responsibilities, she wouldn't have allowed herself to be tempted by this man.

His life was so far removed from hers, it was laughable.

She could just imagine his reaction if she were to invite him to the ball. His polite refusal would no doubt become her second most embarrassing moment ever, after being overheard discussing sex with Anna.

'I'll see you in a minute, Mr Lucarelli.' She lifted the bag that had slipped off her shoulder and his eyes narrowed.

'*Stefano,*' he purred in a disturbingly male voice. 'My name is Stefano. Why does everyone keep calling me Mr Lucarelli? The emergency department is a very informal place to work.'

'Well, you're extremely senior and you're also relatively new so I suppose people are wary about being too familiar, and some people find you—' She broke off and backed towards the staffroom. 'I really need to change.'

'Wait.' His fingers closed over her arm. 'You didn't finish your sentence. Some people find me…?'

She hesitated. 'Intimidating. Just a little.'

'Intimidating? Me?' His dark eyes were lazily amused. 'I'm a pussycat.'

'Technically, so is a tiger,' Liv said dryly and he laughed.

'Providing people do their jobs correctly, I promise to keep my claws sheathed.' His gaze lingered on her face. 'You say "some people". Not you?'

Did he know that he was still holding her arm? 'I like the fact you have high standards. It means you're one less thing I have to worry about when I'm in Resus. I'm a control freak.'

He laughed. 'Likewise.'

'Two control freaks working in the same room could be a disaster.'

His eyes narrowed thoughtfully. 'Not if they were working towards the same objective. That would make them a powerful team, I think.' He sounded impossibly Italian and she sucked in a breath and eased her arm away from his grip.

'I'd better get changed or they'll be wondering where I am.'

Liv took refuge in the staffroom, slung her bag in the locker, quickly changed into her uniform and stared at herself in the mirror.

Her heart was thumping and her arm was tingling where he'd touched her.

Take a look at yourself, she told herself, standing square to the mirror. *Remember who you are*. Twenty-eight-year-old single mother. Nothing special. Now remember who he is. Extremely good-looking rich guy with a taste for skinny actresses.

Get a grip, Liv.

CHAPTER FOUR

IT WAS past ten o'clock before Stefano was finally able to leave the emergency department.

It had been a chaotic evening, with two serious car accidents in quick succession placing enormous demands on the already overstretched staff.

Fortunately for him, Liv had been working in Resus with him and things had run amazingly smoothly.

As he walked across the car park, the ground sparkled with frost and the sky was clear enough to warn him that it was going to be another cold night. Mentally he braced himself for a spate of accidents in the morning as drivers hit black ice.

From across the car park came the splutter and cough of an engine that didn't want to start and he saw Liv sitting in a small car, her scarf wrapped tightly around her neck, her breath forming clouds in the cold air.

Stefano tensed, instinctively suspicious.

On at least two occasions in the past, women had faked car problems in order to wangle a lift home with him.

He took a closer look at the car and decided that this particular bout of engine trouble couldn't possibly be anything but genuine. The car was ancient and there was a significant amount of rust at the base of the door. He wasn't surprised that it wouldn't start. What surprised him was that she'd managed to drive it to the hospital in the first place.

Stefano strode across to her and pulled open the door, amazed that it didn't come off in his hand. 'Problems?' He waited for her to give a sigh of relief and ask him for a lift, but instead she just shook her head.

'I'm fine,' she said firmly. 'But thanks for asking. Have a good evening, Mr Lucarelli. See you tomorrow.'

Fine? See you tomorrow? Astounded by her reaction, Stefano rested an arm on the top of the driver's door and leaned down so that he could talk to her properly. 'That engine doesn't sound fine to me.'

He should walk away. She was encouraging him to walk away.

So why didn't he do just that?

'It's a little temperamental, that's all. It likes to keep me guessing.' With a determined look on her face, she turned the key in the ignition again. The car gave a feeble cough and then there was nothing.

'Liv, there's temperamental and there's dead. Your engine is dead.'

'It can't be.' She slumped in her seat, a desperate look in her eyes. 'It just hates cold weather, that's all. If I leave it for a moment, it will start.'

Her teeth were chattering, her lips had a bluish tinge and Stefano reached into the car and gently removed the keys from her frozen fingers. 'This car is *not* going to start. I'll give you a lift wherever you want to go.' He wondered what it was about this particular woman that made him say things he wouldn't normally dream of saying.

But instead of accepting his offer with relief and gratitude, she shook her head firmly.

'Absolutely not.' She gathered her things together. 'I'll be fine, Mr Lucarelli, honestly. But thanks for checking on me. I'm sure you have somewhere you need to be. Please don't hang around on my account.'

She was refusing his offer of help?

Finding himself in completely unknown territory, Stefano didn't know whether to be amused or exasperated. 'And what do you plan to do? Sleep here until your next shift?'

'I'll take the underground. The train runs very close to my house.'

Her black coat was at least two sizes too big, but he caught a glimpse of slim legs in black tights and black boots. She looked more like a teenager than a mother with a young child. 'You're not taking the train.' The thought of her travelling on the underground horrified him. 'I'm giving you a lift.' He leaned across her, swiftly undid her seat belt and gently tugged her out of the car.

'Mr Lucarelli, I really don't—'

'It's Stefano.' He locked her car, not because he thought anyone was likely to steal it—*no one would be that desperate*—but out of consideration for her feelings. 'And you may think you're controlling, but you can't be as controlling as me. If I don't get my own way, I'm unbearable. Ask my sister if you don't believe me. Leave the car. Your garage can sort it out.'

'I don't think so.' Her expression was one of utter desolation and he frowned.

'It's just a car, Liv.'

For a moment she didn't answer and then she looked up at him, her smile just a little too bright. 'Yes, I know. Absolutely. And thanks for the offer of a lift, but I'll be fine on the train.' She eased her arm away from his and he felt a flash of exasperation.

'Do you always refuse help?'

'I'm never usually offered help. I'm used to doing things on my own. Taking care of myself. I suppose I feel…awkward. I don't want to put you out.'

He wondered why she was so suddenly so lacking in confidence when an hour earlier she'd been saving a life. 'So let me get this straight. You would rather skid along an icy pavement in freezing conditions and then wait on a draughty platform for a dark smelly underground train than have a lift to your door in my warm car. I confess I'm not flattered by your choice. Am I really that intimidating?'

Liv's glance was self-conscious. 'You can't possibly want to give me a lift home.'

Faced with the unusual situation of having to persuade a woman into his car, Stefano applied the full force of his personality. 'Just get in the car, Liv, and stop arguing.'

'You're right, you are controlling.'

'In this weather, it's an advantage. *Accidenti*, we're both going to freeze.' He took her hand and led her across the car park, noticing that her fingers were very slim and very cold. 'You should wear gloves.'

'I lost them.' She snatched her hand away from his as if she had only just realised that he was holding her. Immediately she slipped on the ice and would have crashed to the ground if he hadn't caught her. 'Oops! Oh my goodness!' Her legs slithered and he held her firmly, gritting his teeth as he felt the brush of her body against his.

Liv started to giggle and her laughter was so infectious that he found himself smiling, too.

'Stefano.' He held her firmly as she struggled to regain her footing on the icy surface. 'My name is Stefano. Start using it or I'll drop you.'

'If you drop me, you'll end up fixing the damage. You can let go of me now, I'm fine.' Gingerly her fingers released their grip on the front of his coat. 'Thank you.'

He tried to ignore the scent of her hair and the way her soft curves pressed against him, but the reaction of his body was instantaneous and he was experienced enough to know that the astonishing chemistry wasn't all on his side.

Her cheeks were pink and she was looking everywhere except at him.

Definitely not all on his side.

Wondering why she was so determined to get away from him when the attraction between them was so powerful, he reluctantly released her. 'Let's get in the car before we both develop hypothermia. Give me directions to your house.'

Her eyes slid over his car, the streamlined black Ferrari that had been his Christmas present to himself two years previously. 'All right, now I'm envious. Your car has no rust and I bet the engine starts first time.'

'Actually it doesn't.' Stefano opened the door. 'It hates the cold damp weather. I'm starting to think I should garage it over the winter and—' He had been about to say 'and use the other car' when he'd realised how insensitive that would be in the circumstances. 'Get in, Liv, before we both freeze.'

With obvious reluctance, she did as she was told and he strode round the car and settled himself in the driver's seat.

With an unconsciously sensual movement, she slid her hands slowly over the leather seats and her eyes flickered to the dashboard. 'Four point three litre engine,' she murmured, 'Naught to sixty in 3.9 seconds, F1 paddle shift transmission and carbon ceramic composite brakes.'

Stefano stared at her in incredulous disbelief and she smiled at him.

'Modified version of the 360s semi-space frame aluminium chassis. Capable of a top speed of 196 miles per hour.'

Stefano drew some much-needed air into his lungs. 'You're interested in cars?'

'Not in the slightest, but don't tell my little boy. He thinks I love cars.' Her eyes danced and her cheeks dimpled. 'I'm living proof that it's possible to sound knowledgeable about a subject without actually understanding anything. All I really know about your car is that it can go fast. Which isn't much use in London.'

Stefano started to laugh. 'You memorised all that?'

'Well, not intentionally. But Max doesn't like fairy-tales much. He prefers to read about engines and how things work. Anna's husband gave him a book on super-cars.'

'So you curl up in bed at night reading about Ferraris?'

'Gripping, don't you think? I can hardly wait to turn the page. Next week we should be moving on to Lamborghini. I particularly enjoyed November because that was Maserati.'

He loved her sense of humour but most of all he liked her smile. She was smiling at him now and it took all his willpower not to bring his mouth down on hers because the curve of her lips was so, so tempting.

But there was no sign of flirtation. Nothing to suggest she was even aware of her own appeal or the effect she was having on him.

'Your little boy is very lucky,' he said softly and her smile dimmed slightly.

'Not really. He's crazy about cars and football. I've done a great deal of homework on both subjects but it isn't really the same.' Staring at the monitors on the dashboard, she looked suddenly wistful. 'My own bedtime reading is a book on coaching football. Max is desperate to make the first team.'

He could imagine her studying the book, trying to help her little boy. 'He played today, so your coaching has obviously paid off.'

'I wish that were true, but I'm afraid it isn't. I think he has a natural talent but I have no idea how to foster that talent,' she admitted. 'I need to get some practical advice from somewhere. This afternoon all these fathers were yelling technical stuff to their boys and—' She broke off and shot him an apologetic glance. 'Sorry. This is very boring for you.'

He'd never been less bored by a woman in his life. 'I'm sure that the important thing for Max was that you were actually there, supporting him. Where is his father? Does he ever come and watch him?' He leaned across and fastened her seat belt, feeling her shrink against the seat as his hands brushed against her body.

She snuggled deeper inside the coat and he wondered why she was so self-conscious.

'I have no idea where his father is,' she croaked, her cheeks a little pinker than they had been a few moments before. 'Off enjoying himself somewhere, I should imagine. I'm not married, Mr Lucarelli. Nor do I want to be,' she said hastily and he hid a smile because she was obviously concerned that he might misinterpret her unguarded declaration.

He thought of Francine, who could have turned flirtation into an Olympic sport. Then he glanced at Liv's sweet profile and suddenly wanted to know more about her.

'You're not in touch with his father?'

'Jack was allergic to children. Unfortunately for Max, I didn't discover that until after I became pregnant.'

'He knew you were pregnant and he left you?' Unable to hide his disapproval, Stefano frowned and she cleared her throat.

'Not immediately. He hung around until Max was three. Sort of.'

'Sort of?' Uncomprehending, Stefano glanced at her but she was staring straight ahead.

'Well, we were married but not really…together. He had someone else, but I didn't find out for quite a while. Actually he had quite a few "someone elses" which doesn't do much for one's confidence, obviously. And I can't believe I'm telling you this.' She glanced at him, appalled. 'Why am I telling you this?'

'Because I asked.'

'Well that will teach you not to ask.' She looked away. 'It was all my fault, anyway.'

'*How* was it your fault?'

'I wasn't his type. I should have seen that right at the beginning,' she said quickly. 'Jack was handsome and clever.'

Not that clever, Stefano thought grimly, glancing at her profile and wondering if she realised just how much she'd revealed about herself with that simple statement. 'He wanted nothing to do with his son?'

It was a few seconds before she answered. 'No.'

'But he gives you financial help?'

Liv turned her head and stared out of the window. 'Do you think we should get going before the temperature drops any further? The roads will be lethal. I can't remember much about the Ferrari's performance on sheet ice.'

Stefano sat still for a moment, interpreting her answer.

So that was why she was so worried about her car.

It was obvious that she had no financial help and she was raising a child in an expensive city on a nurse's meagre salary. She was doing it all on her own. All of it.

But that didn't really explain why Anna had been talking about Liv's apparently non-existent sex life. Why wasn't she dating? Silently contemplating that issue, he started the engine and reversed out of his space. 'So who is looking after Max now? Do you have a nanny?'

'I use a childminder before and after school, but tonight he's doing a sleepover at Anna's. Max is best friends with her little boy.'

'So you're not rushing home to him?'

'No. Why?'

Making an instantaneous decision, Stefano steered the car down a series of back streets and then pulled in and parked. 'Because it means we have time to grab something to eat before I drop you home. Neither of us has eaten since lunchtime. You must be starving and there is an absolutely fantastic Italian restaurant here.'

'No!' Liv swivelled to face him, her expression horrified. 'It's incredibly kind of you, but I couldn't possibly do that.'

'Why not?'

'Because— No.' Her gaze slid from his. 'I'll make myself some toast before I go to bed.'

'Toast?' Having never eaten toast for dinner in his life, Stefano looked at her in amazement. 'I'm suggesting we go out to eat and you're choosing toast?'

'Yes.'

'Why?'

'Loads of reasons.' She fiddled with the strap of her handbag, her discomfort so acute that it was almost painful to watch. 'I'm not dressed for a fancy restaurant and I can't afford to eat out.'

The change in her was startling. Working with him in Resus she'd been a poised, confident professional, but faced with a trip to a restaurant she'd become a shy, awkward woman. And she wasn't even looking him in the eye.

Instinctively taking control, Stefano reached across and

undid her seat belt, noticing the way she flattened herself against the seat again. 'It isn't fancy and this is my treat. A thank-you for having made my life easier in the department.

'Mr Lucarelli, I really can't—'

'Liv, I'm buying you a bowl of spaghetti, that's all.' He'd never before had to persuade a woman to have dinner with him and she was obviously well aware of that fact because she shot him an agonised look.

'There must be someone else you can take!' Her tone bordered on the desperate and he gave a faint smile.

'You're not doing much for my ego. Is the thought of facing me across a bowl of spaghetti really that terrifying?'

'No! It isn't you, it's me. I'm just not—' She broke off, clearly finding the situation painfully awkward. 'I'm not very exciting company, that's all.'

Accustomed to being with women who were confident both socially and sexually, it took him a moment to adjust to the contrast.

He studied her face in silence, taking in the self-doubt in her eyes and the touch of colour in her cheeks. 'Liv, what is the matter with you? Do you really expect me to believe that you can handle the most demanding medical emergency with total confidence but can't wind spaghetti onto a fork and talk at the same time?'

She gave a reluctant laugh. 'I suppose it's all about practice. I'm more confident at Resus-speak than dinner-table-speak.'

'Fine, then we'll talk about pelvic fractures. Or we won't talk at all. I really don't care, just as long as I eat something in the next five minutes.' He extracted her from the car and propelled her, still protesting, through the door of the restaurant.

They were instantly enveloped by warmth and delicious

smells and Liv hesitated on the threshold, scanning the room like a gazelle sensing danger.

All evidence of the cool professional had left her and she looked so painfully unsure of herself that for a moment Stefano thought she might actually turn and run. He planted himself behind her, watching as she took in the cheerful red tablecloths, the enormous Christmas tree and the cosy, informality of the place.

Then she turned her head and gave him a hesitant smile. 'It's nice.'

'*Sì*, I know. Just wait until you taste the pasta. It's incredible.' Stefano tried to peel the coat from her shoulders, but she clutched at it self consciously.

'I'll keep it on. I'm not dressed to go out to dinner,' she muttered and he gently but firmly uncurled her fingers.

'You can't eat dinner in your coat. This is a very informal place.' He prised the coat from her grip and handed it to the waiter. 'No one dresses up to come here and anyway, you look fine.'

She looked a lot better than fine. Without the protection of the coat he could see that her legs went on for ever and the way that her skinny rib jumper clung to her gorgeous curves drew the attention of several men in the room, but he decided that to comment on her appearance would just make her even more uncomfortable.

She obviously had no idea how attractive she was.

Which made a refreshing change from the women he usually mixed with, he thought wryly, recalling Francine's endless preoccupation with her own reflection.

Not wanting to risk increasing Liv's anxiety levels by offering her a menu, he turned to the owner and spoke in rapid Italian, telling him where they wanted to sit and what they wanted to eat.

The owner led them to a quiet table by the window and Liv gave a soft gasp of delight.

'We're right next to the river here—I didn't realise. It's so pretty, especially in the dark when it's all lit up and you can't see the dirt.'

'This restaurant is a hidden gem. I discovered it on a trip to London a few years ago. Because you approach it via all the back streets, you don't realise that it's by the Thames. What can I get you to drink? Champagne?'

'Champagne?' Startled, she dragged her eyes away from the view and looked at him. 'No thanks, water will be fine.'

'Water?'

'I did warn you that I'm incredibly boring.' Reaching for her napkin, she spread it on her lap. 'Champagne is for women who don't have to get up at five in the morning.'

'You get up at five?'

'If I don't start then, I can't get everything done.'

A waiter placed two heaped bowls of spaghetti bolognese in front of them and Liv glanced at him in surprise. 'I didn't know you'd ordered.'

'This is the best thing on the menu and it's just what you need after a day on your feet. Eat.' He picked up his fork and then suddenly wondered if he'd ordered the wrong thing for her. 'Just leave the pasta and eat the sauce, if you prefer.'

This time she laughed, her green eyes sparkling in the candlelight. 'I think you're definitely confused about who you're having dinner with.' She spiralled pasta onto her fork like a professional. 'I'm a working mother, Stefano. If I don't eat carbohydrates, I collapse. Anyway, I'm starving and this smells delicious. I couldn't leave any of it if you paid me.'

Stefano watched her eat the first mouthful and felt an explosion of heat through his loins. 'You must have Italian genes.'

'No, I have a son who loves spaghetti. It's Max's second favourite gourmet treat.'

'His first being?'

'Pizza. He'd eat it every night if I let him. We make it together, from scratch. There's nothing quite like kneading dough to let off steam after a hard day.' Gradually she relaxed with him and he kept the conversation flowing, deriving immense satisfaction from the fact that she seemed to have lost her earlier awkwardness.

Soon she was telling him all the details of her life. They talked about work, about living in London and she mentioned Max a lot, recounting several anecdotes that made him laugh.

'It must be pretty tiring, working a full day and then going home and being a mum.' The amount she did in a day stunned him. 'I don't suppose you have much time to yourself.'

'I don't really want that,' she said simply. 'I love being with him. He's fun. We have a nice time together. And once he's asleep I have time to myself.'

And then she read books on coaching football.

'So you basically work all day and spend time with your seven-year-old.' *Was that why Anna had been offering to buy her hot sex for Christmas?* Stefano reached for some more bread. 'Do you ever go out?'

'Oh yes, we often go to one of the museums at the weekend and sometimes we'll go to the cinema for a treat. He loves it and so do I.'

That wasn't what he'd meant, but he didn't push her.

Clearly her life was her work and her child and Stefano finished his spaghetti and lounged in his chair, listening as she talked about her hectic life and her hopes for Max. He was intrigued by how happy she seemed. 'So is Max looking forward to Christmas?'

'Yes. Not that we do much. Turkey, presents, trip to the park…' She shrugged and added, 'Last year we went on a trip to the seaside and played on the beach. Freezing but fun. I try and do a special trip, to make up for the fact it's just the two of us.'

'You don't have family?'

'No.' She concentrated on her plate. 'I only have one aunt and she lives in Scotland so I never get to see her. What about you? Will you be spending Christmas with your family?'

'Yes. I have an interfering younger sister, an even more interfering father and at least eight first cousins.'

'Lucky you.' Her tone was wistful. 'I imagine there's nothing better than a noisy, chaotic Christmas when everyone is driving everyone else mad.'

'You think that's lucky?'

Liv reached for her water. 'I suppose that the fact they interfere at least means they care. And it's lovely to have someone who cares. The world can be a lonely, scary place.'

Did she find it scary? *Was she lonely?*

Sensing that to delve deeper into that comment might send her back into her shell, Stefano shifted the conversation. 'My sister has twin boys the same age as Max.'

'Really?' Her face brightened. 'That must be a handful. I can't imagine two.'

'She has a nanny. My sister works in the family business.'

Liv studied him across the table, her green eyes reflecting the flickering candlelight. 'And you disapprove of that?'

'The children need her. And she doesn't need to work.'

'I presume you mean financially. But maybe she needs to work for other reasons.'

'Let me ask you a question.' He wondered how he could ever have thought she wasn't beautiful. Her face had a pure, innocent quality but her mouth had been designed for seduction. 'If you had all the money you needed, would you still work?'

'I have no idea. I've never thought about it and I wouldn't allow myself to because it isn't an option for me. Happiness is being realistic, Stefano.'

Noticing that she was trying not to yawn, he caught the eye of the waiter. 'Time to get you home.'

'Sorry. It was a bit of an early start this morning.' Her attention was on a different part of the restaurant and when he followed her gaze he saw that a table of women were all watching him and laughing. They were obviously enjoying a girls' night out and one of them lifted her glass and sent a flirtatious look in his direction.

Stefano didn't react, but Liv's friendly, open chatter suddenly ceased and she returned to looking awkward and uncomfortable, her eyes on the view instead of him.

Why was she so self-conscious?

She'd retreated back into her shell and he knew that her reaction had something to do with the noisy group of women who were partying at the nearby table.

He was unable to retrieve the situation because the waiter arrived with the bill and stood hovering while Stefano produced his credit card.

'Tell me how much my half is,' Liv said huskily. 'I'll pay you back tomorrow. I'm so sorry I don't have enough money with me now.'

Amused, he glanced at her. 'When I buy a woman dinner, I don't expect her to pay.'

'Maybe not, but that's when you're on a date and this wasn't a date. This was just two colleagues sharing food. I'll pay you back tomorrow.'

The money was obviously an enormous issue for her and

he wondered how, if she was really so short of cash, she was ever going to get her car fixed. 'I don't want you to pay me back. I was hungry and there's nothing more grim than eating alone. You did me a favour.'

'Hardly. I talked far too much about really boring subjects.' Clearly in a hurry to leave, she rose to her feet and didn't speak again until they reached the car. 'Thank you, Stefano.'

'Give me directions to your flat.' He steered the conversation away from money. 'Have you worked in the emergency department for long?'

'The last few years. Before that I was on Paediatrics and sometimes when they're short staffed I still go and help there. What about you? Where did you work last?'

'In a trauma unit up in Scotland and before that Milan.'

'Milan.' She repeated the word with the same emphasis he'd used. 'That sounds exotic.'

Stefano laughed. 'If you think that, you have clearly never been to Milan.'

'I've never been anywhere. Take a left at the lights. And then it's straight on all the way to my flat. Just keep going. So what's Milan like?'

'It's a wonderful city, but I wouldn't describe it as exotic.'

'Why did you choose to come to frozen England?'

'I needed a change.' And this was certainly a change, he thought grimly, scanning the streets. As she directed him, the area he was driving through grew more and more rundown. There was litter on the streets, graffiti on the walls and gangs of teenagers wearing hoodies lurked on street corners.

'You were escaping from your interfering family?'

'Something like that.' His family and a clingy ex-girlfriend. A police car raced past them, light flashing, horn blaring, and Stefano felt the tension in his shoulders mount. He wouldn't want any of his family living in a place like this.

'We're here,' she said a few minutes later. 'If you pull in just past that lamppost, that's my flat. Thanks very much.' As the car drew to a halt, she reached for her bag. 'I really am grateful. The meal was delicious and you've been very kind. See you tomorrow.'

One glance at the area told him that she shouldn't be coming back here late at night on her own. 'Wait.' His hand on her arm prevented her leaving the car. 'I'll see you to your door.'

'There's really no need. I know it looks grim but I'm used to it.' Not looking at him, Liv produced her keys. 'I'll be fine.'

'You're very independent, aren't you?'

'I've had to be.' She glanced at him then and their eyes met and held. Then she gave a tiny frown and tore her gaze away from his. 'Goodnight, Mr Lucarelli. And thanks again.'

The chemistry was shimmering between them like an invisible force and yet her hand slid to the door.

'Invite me in for coffee.' His softly spoken command obviously surprised her and he watched with some satisfaction as the keys slipped from her fingers. It was nice to know she wasn't indifferent to him. Uncomfortable, yes. Shy, maybe. But indifferent? *Definitely not.* 'You've already told me that Max is at Anna's tonight, so you have no bedtime story to read.' He lounged in his seat, enjoying the effect he was having on her. She was delightfully transparent.

'You don't strike me as the sort of man who'd step out of his Ferrari to drink a cup of instant coffee in a damp flat that is probably smaller than your bathroom,' she said lightly and he gave a slow smile.

'I love instant coffee and I'm nervous in large spaces. I promise to give you a lesson on how to coach football.'

'Now you're being unfair.' She laughed. 'Mr Lucarelli—Stefano.' She stumbled over his name and stooped to retrieve her keys, 'That's a really tempting offer and I really am grateful for the lift, but I've already taken up enough of your Friday evening. I'm sure you have plenty more exciting ways to spend your time than drinking coffee with me.' And before he could answer, she slid out of his car and hurried across to her flat.

Stefano wondered why he was so desperate to follow her.

She had nothing, absolutely nothing, in common with the women he usually spent time with. Obviously her life revolved around her work and her son. It was almost as if she'd forgotten that she was a woman. Or maybe she just ignored that fact.

His eyes narrowed as he remembered the way she'd hung onto her coat in the restaurant. She was woman enough to care that she hadn't dressed to go to a restaurant.

He watched as she hurried up the steps to the front door of her flat, his eyes narrowed and his body aching with awareness. She moved with the grace of a dancer and flakes of snow settled on her dark hair as she fumbled to get her key into the lock.

As the door opened she paused and Stefano waited for her to look back and smile at him.

She was going to look back. He felt it.

She stood for a moment on the threshold and then stepped inside her flat and firmly closed the door behind her.

And she didn't look back.

Liv stood in the kitchen, willing herself not to run to the window and see if his car was still there.

Had she imagined it or had he really invited himself in for coffee?

And why had he done that?

Surely the time they'd spent together in the restaurant should have been enough to prove to him that she wasn't exactly stimulating company. She'd talked about work and Max.

Thinking about how much she'd talked and how boring she'd been, she covered her face with her hands and gave a groan of embarrassment. Not only had she been boring, she'd been wearing her most ancient skirt and jumper. A man like Stefano Lucarelli must be used to being with women who were groomed to within an inch of their lives. And on top of that, she'd cleared her plate. She'd eaten absolutely everything and his comment about just eating the sauce had made it perfectly obvious that he was used to stick-thin women who went to restaurants to be seen, rather than to eat.

He'd offered her champagne!

Thank goodness she'd had the sense to refuse, otherwise the evening would have been even more embarrassing. As it was, he was probably regretting ever offering her a lift. Because of her stupid car, he'd been stuck with her all evening.

And he'd been incredibly kind about it. So kind that for a short time she'd completely forgotten to be shy and awkward and had really enjoyed herself.

After a while she'd even managed to forget how impossibly good-looking he was and how he absolutely shouldn't be wasting an evening on her, and just concentrate on the conversation. And he'd been really, *really* good company. Although she knew it wasn't fashionable to admit it, she loved the fact that he'd just taken charge.

He was *so* sure of himself and confident and wasn't afraid to make decisions. Just having someone else make a decision for her had had the same effect as a month on a health farm.

It was just because she was a single mother, she thought wistfully. Every decision that needed to be made, she made it—by herself, with no help or input from anyone else and sometimes the unrelenting responsibility of her life was just *exhausting*. Yes, she was controlling, but only because she'd had to be. It was hardly surprising that when someone else did the thinking for five minutes, it had felt wonderful.

It had felt so incredibly indulgent to have a plate of food put in front of her that for a short time she'd relaxed and been herself with him. Only she'd talked far too much about her life—it was a wonder he hadn't fallen asleep in his spaghetti.

It was just as well she'd happened to notice the table of women near to them. Made up and dressed up, they'd obviously spent half the day getting ready for their night out and they had gazed at Stefano as though they'd wanted him for their main course.

At that point she'd remembered just who she was with and she'd returned to earth quickly, reminding herself that it wasn't a date.

He'd been with her because he was polite, not because he'd been attracted to her. For a moment in the car the atmosphere had been stretched and tight and she'd thought—she'd really thought that it was caused by mutual attraction and then she'd realised that the tension had simply been caused by him trying to find a tactful way of extracting her from his car.

Why would a man like him be interested in someone as ordinary as her? He just had well-developed social skills, that was all.

He'd only invited her to dinner because he'd been hungry and he'd been forced to give her a lift. It must have been a horribly awkward situation for him.

No wonder he'd suddenly asked for the bill, instead of lingering over dessert and coffee.

He'd obviously been desperate to escape as fast as possible. And for her own sanity, she needed to remember that.

CHAPTER FIVE

'LIV, you're needed in Resus. We've just admitted a woman with chest pains. She had a Caesarean section seven days ago.' Anna removed the keys to the drug cupboard from her pocket. 'By the way, why was your car iced over in the car park this morning?'

'It didn't start last night. Did you say she has just had a baby?'

'That's right. Second baby, six-hour discharge, no problems. How did you get home if your car died?'

'I grabbed a lift.' Without elaborating, Liv hurried into Resus just as the paramedics left the room, pushing the empty stretcher.

'We're going to give you some oxygen to help you breathe, Michelle,' Stefano was saying and he glanced up as Liv joined him by the side of the trolley. For a brief moment his dark eyes lingered on hers and that one look was sufficient to trigger memories of the explicit dreams that had disturbed her sleep the night before.

Remembering just what he'd been doing to her in those dreams, colour flooded into her cheeks and he noted her response with a slight narrowing of his sexy eyes before shifting his gaze back to the radiographer who was hovering. 'We'll do a chest X-ray, although I'm not sure it's going to tell us much.'

'I can't breathe—I'm so worried...' The woman's lips were blue and Liv took her hand and gave it a gentle squeeze, trying to ignore the increase in her own heart rate.

It had just been a dream, for goodness' sake. A dream he knew nothing about. Unless he could read minds, he was never going to find out that she'd been having totally inappropriate fantasies about him.

Angry with herself, Liv checked the monitor. 'Pulse is a hundred and fifteen.'

It was totally ridiculous to feel like this. He'd given her a lift home, that was all. Trying to forget about the previous evening, she concentrated her attention on the patient. 'How are those pains, Michelle?'

Michelle closed her eyes. 'Worse when I breathe.'

Liv's immediate thought was that the woman had suffered a pulmonary embolus, a clot in her lung. She looked at Stefano and he gave a brief nod of agreement, clearly reading her mind.

At least in the emergency department they were completely in tune.

'You're in hospital now, so try to leave the worrying to us, Michelle.' Liv glanced over her shoulder to one of the other nurses. 'Alice? Can you call the obstetric unit and see if they can track down her notes, please?'

'I've left my husband with the kids.' Gasping for breath, the woman was clearly frantic with worry. 'The baby's only a week old and I'm breastfeeding. He's never going to cope.'

'Is he coming to the hospital?' Liv watched as Stefano prepared to take blood from the radial artery, his fingers swift and confident.

Michelle coughed feebly. 'He's supposed to be following in the car.'

'I'm just going to take some blood from your wrist, Michelle,' Stefano murmured. 'This might hurt a bit.'

'I'm worried that the baby is going to be starving.' Tears welled up in Michelle's eyes. 'She has no idea how to take a bottle. Ow.' She screwed up her face. 'You're right, that does hurt.'

'*Mi dispiace.* I'm sorry. I know it's uncomfortable.' Stefano straightened. 'I want her catheterised so that we can monitor her fluid output. Let's give her some high-flow oxygen and we need to get a line in. Phil, I want FBC, ESR and U&Es. She has pleuritic chest pain and a pleural rub.' He delivered a string of commands, his instructions succinct and fluent and Liv stood back for a moment so that the radiographer could do her job.

'We're just going to run a few tests on you, Michelle, and then I promise I'll go and talk to your husband. If necessary I can fetch someone from the obstetric unit to help with the baby.'

Michelle pressed a hand to her chest, her breath coming in shallow pants. 'I've never felt anything like this before. It feels as though I'm being stabbed.'

'The chest X-ray looks completely normal,' Phil muttered and Stefano's dark eyes flickered to the screen. For a brief moment all his attention was focused on the image and everyone in the room looked at him expectantly.

Liv glanced at the monitor again. 'Sats are dropping,' she murmured and reached for the ECG machine.

'The clinical signs are all consistent with a diagnosis of PE,' Stefano reached out a hand to take a set of results that one of the nurses was flourishing in his direction. He scanned them quickly and then put them on top of the notes. 'She's seven days post-Caesarean section, which is a major risk factor. Let's give her a dose of tinzaparin.'

Liv checked Michelle's blood pressure again. 'Her pulse is a hundred and ten and she's hypotensive.' She turned back to the patient. 'Michelle, I just want to do a trace of your heart so I'm going to undo your shirt and attach some wires to your chest.'

'Has my husband arrived?' Michelle's breathing was shallow and rapid. 'Could you find out? It's really worrying me.'

'Rachel?' Liv spoke over her shoulder. 'Can you go to the desk and ask them to tell us as soon as Michelle's family arrive? Put them in the relatives' room and make sure they have everything they need. I'll be with them as soon as I can.'

Michelle gave a strangled laugh. 'I can't be in hospital. I have a new baby and it's Christmas in a couple of weeks.'

'Don't worry about that, now,' Liv soothed, her eyes on the ECG. 'Stefano?'

'*Sì*, I am looking.' His eyes narrowed, he studied the trace. 'Get ICU on the phone for me. And I want 10 milligrams of alteplase as a starting dose. Let's arrange for a CT scan.'

It was another hour before Michelle was finally transferred to ICU and only then did Liv and Stefano go and talk to her husband.

They found him pacing the relatives' room, holding a bawling baby against his shoulder while a toddler clung to his leg.

'How is she? The other nurse said she was being transferred.' White-faced with anxiety, he stepped towards Stefano and the baby's screams intensified, as if the infant sensed that something important was happening. The father rubbed her back helplessly. 'Sorry. I'm so sorry. I don't know what to do with her. I think she's hungry and I can't get her to take the bottle. Michelle expressed some milk last night and left it in the fridge, so it isn't that it tastes different but I think she just isn't used to the teat, or something.'

'Why don't I have a try?' Liv held out her arms. 'Then you

can have a proper conversation with Mr Lucarelli. I'm sure there are lots of things you want to ask him.'

'Would you mind?' Gently and slightly clumsily he lifted the baby from his shoulder and handed her to Liv. 'You forget how tiny they are when they're first born. It's terrifying.'

Liv expertly snuggled the baby against her and reached for the bottle, leaving Stefano to update Nick on his wife's condition.

She sat down in the chair, settled the baby in the crook of her arm and drew the teat across her lips. 'You poor little thing,' she murmured softly. 'Are you starving?'

The baby was red-faced from crying and gave a little hiccough. Then she played with the teat for a moment before turning her head away in disgust.

'I know it feels a bit weird, but it tastes just the same. Trust me.' Liv squeezed a tiny bit of the milk onto the baby's lips and watched as her mouth moved hungrily. 'See? It tastes nice. We just need to teach you to suck.' She skilfully manoeuvred the teat into the baby's mouth and the infant lay still for a moment, and then gave a gulp and swallowed. Liv smiled. 'Good girl.'

'Oh thank goodness,' Nick muttered, watching from across the room. 'She's been crying for hours. I was at my wits' end. You are utterly, utterly amazing.'

Liv glanced up and met Stefano's eyes and there was something in his watchful gaze that made her shift awkwardly in her seat.

What was he thinking?

Probably that she was good with babies but hopeless at scintillating dinner conversation.

Still mortified that she'd gone on and on the night before, she dipped her head and concentrated on the baby. 'She's fine. She just needed a bit of help to suck from a teat. It's a different technique.'

Nick gave a helpless shrug. 'I don't suppose you fancy moving in with me for a week or so?'

Liv gently withdrew the bottle from the baby's mouth and lifted the baby against her shoulder. 'What about Grandma? Can she help?'

'She's great with this one...' Nick scooped the toddler onto his lap '...but the baby needs Michelle.'

Stefano rose to his feet. 'Let's see how she goes this morning. Once her condition is stabilised we may be able to transfer her to a ward and she can have the baby with her. We'll do everything we can to help, I assure you.'

'You've been very kind.'

The door opened and Anna put her head round the door. 'Liv? Can Rachel take over in there so that you can help me out here? Everyone is obviously bored with Christmas shopping so they've decided to spend the afternoon with us instead.'

'No problem.' Liv carefully handed the baby back to Nick and smiled at him. 'You can stay here for now. Once we have some news from ICU, you can go and see Michelle.'

She left the room and hurried after Anna but Stefano's fingers curled around her wrist and stopped her.

'Liv, wait.'

The touch of his hand turned her limbs to jelly and she took several deep breaths before turning to face him. This time she was *not* going to embarrass herself. 'Thank you for last night,' she said brightly, staring at a point in the middle of his chest. 'Best spaghetti I've ever eaten. Oh—here's the money I owe you.' She dug twenty pounds out of her pocket, trying not to think what that bowl of spaghetti had done to her budget.

'I don't want your money, Liv.' His voice was a deep, lazy

drawl and the breath stuck in her throat because he was so cool and in control and she felt so, so awkward.

'Please take it. Honestly. There's no reason why you should pay for me.' She risked a glance at him and then wished she hadn't because he was the sort of man you just couldn't look away from. He was impossibly, indecently handsome and his gaze held hers for a moment and then flickered to her mouth.

Liv stopped breathing and a slow, dangerous warmth spread through her body. For a wickedly delicious moment she thought he might actually be wondering what it would be like to kiss her.

And then she returned to reality.

Boring.

His eyes narrowed. 'What would be boring?'

Horrified, Liv stared at him. *Had she really spoken her thoughts aloud?* 'Nothing. Take the money.' She pushed it into his hand and started to back away. 'I really have to go. Anna needs me, and—'

'Liv, stop it.' His eyes were amused. 'Why are you so jumpy? Last night over dinner you managed to relax and be yourself. For the first time I actually had a glimpse of the real you.'

Liv almost groaned. 'Yes, I know,' she muttered, 'and I'm really, *really* sorry about that. I suppose it's because I don't often find myself in adult company, apart from with the patients and they don't count. I was a little carried away talking about my life. No wonder you only ordered one course.'

Surprise flickered in his eyes and he watched her for a moment, his expression thoughtful. 'I ordered one course because most of the women I take out to dinner don't eat anything,' he said softly and she gave a resigned smile.

If she'd needed a reminder that she bore no resemblance to the type of woman he usually dated, she had it now. 'Well, you only have to look at me to know that I'm not in that category—but then you weren't really taking me out to dinner, were you? It was more a question of me gatecrashing and—' she broke off and studied his face. 'Why are you smiling?'

'Because you fascinate me. In Resus you are always cool and in control. You are fast, bright and confident. And then we leave Resus and you are a nervous wreck. Why is that, I wonder?'

The way he was looking at her made her feel hot and shivery at the same time.

'I...really ought to go, because...' horribly out of her depth, she waved a hand vaguely. 'I...just really ought to go.' Why was he talking to her, anyway? Why was he bothering?

'Give me your car keys.'

'My—' She frowned. 'Why?'

'Because someone from my garage is coming to pick up your car in ten minutes.'

Liv stared at him in astonishment. 'Your garage? But they fix Ferraris.'

'They're skilled mechanics.' Stefano inclined his head as the neurology consultant wandered past and muttered a greeting. 'They can fix anything with an engine.'

'I'm not sure that mine even falls into that category,' Liv joked weakly, incredibly touched that he'd offered. *Why? Why had he offered?* 'I couldn't possibly say yes. Even if they could fix it, they'd charge a fortune. Garages take one look at me and rip me off.'

'All the more reason to let me sort this one out. Garages don't rip me off.' His tone was pleasant but there was a hard glint in his eyes that made her smile.

'I imagine they wouldn't dare.' Panic fluttered inside her when she thought about all the demands on her meagre salary. 'I suppose I could use the Christmas-tree money.' She murmured those words to herself and Stefano raised an eyebrow in question.

'The Christmas-tree money?'

Trying to work out how to find a Christmas tree that didn't cost anything, Liv felt her head start to throb. 'Look, I hadn't expected my car to die three weeks before Christmas, which obviously wasn't very sensible planning on my part, but there you are. I basically can't afford to get it fixed yet.' What was the point in pretending? It was obvious from the state of her car that she wasn't rolling in money. 'But thanks for offering.'

'How much is your budget?'

'A hundred pounds.' Saying it aloud, it sounded so ridiculous that Liv started to laugh. 'You see? It's hopeless. I doubt they'd even tow it away for that.'

'It might not be anything too serious. Let's wait and see what they say. My mechanic is cheap and reliable.' His eyes lingered on her face and she felt her insides heat.

'I don't know what to say.'

'You say yes.'

Faced with the tempting vision of a problem solved, Liv felt herself waver. 'If it's more than a hundred pounds—'

'Then I'll tell them not to do the work. Now give me the keys.' He held out his hand. 'Keys, Liv.'

She handed them over. 'I don't know why you're helping me.'

'I know you don't.' With that enigmatic comment, he strolled away from her, her car keys in his hand, leaving her staring after him in bemusement.

'I don't care how much it costs.' Stefano trawled through his emails as he made the call. 'I just want it fixed. Fast. And I want the bill to say £102.' He listened for a moment as the mechanic outlined the dire state of Liv's car. 'Yes, I know all that. I have eyes… I don't care about that, either… A new engine—yes, whatever, and there's one other thing.' He frowned as he scanned the email from the chief executive demanding his presence at a meeting on cost-cutting. 'I want you to deliver a hire car here this afternoon. A new, safe hatchback, nothing too flashy.' Having sorted out that problem, he terminated the call and turned to the pile of letters on his desk, but he was called to see a patient and then another and it was several hours before he was finally able to return to the mounting paperwork.

He was just trying to work up some enthusiasm for an extremely dry memo from the Department of Health when there was a tap on the door.

Liv stood there, a set of keys in her hand. 'The garage delivered me a car,' she gasped. 'Did you arrange it?'

Stefano relaxed back in his chair, watching her. 'They always give a complimentary car. Perhaps I forgot to mention that.'

'When they're servicing your Ferrari, maybe, but *not* when they're given an ancient rust bucket to resuscitate.'

'It's Christmas. I told them that you have a child and that you work at the hospital. People are extra-kind to nurses and rightly so. Just accept it, Liv.' His order was met by silence and she simply stared at him. Then she gave a little sob and suddenly burst into tears.

Appalled, Stefano rose to his feet. '*Accidenti*, who has upset you? Tell me and I will sort it out right now!'

'No one. Nothing. I'm sorry.' She rubbed the palm of her hand across one cheek and then the other, wiping away the tears, visibly struggling to pull herself together. 'It's just that I'm not used to—I usually have to sort out everything myself. I'm not used to people being kind and—I can't believe you persuaded them to lend me a car.' Her voice cracked. 'Thank you. Thank you so much.'

Frozen to the spot, Stefano watched her, uncertain how to respond. Usually female tears left him cold, but he'd never encountered the genuine article before. Neither had he ever been so profusely thanked for so small a gesture. He'd once given Francine a diamond necklace, but even that extravagant gift had merited little more than a loud squeal and a comment that matching earrings would have been nice.

'You're welcome,' he said softly and Liv gave him an embarrassed smile and pulled a tissue out of her pocket.

'I seem to make a habit of making a fool of myself in front of you.' She blew her nose hard. 'You're probably thinking I'm a complete psycho.'

He thought she was delightfully natural, refreshingly honest and achingly sexy. 'I think you're tired, and that is hardly surprising given how hard you work.'

'I like my work.'

And in her time off, she read to her child. Books on cars and football.

He'd never met anyone as selfless as her. Sensing that she was struggling for control, Stefano shifted the subject away from the personal. 'I just spoke to ICU. Michelle is stable.'

Liv's face brightened. 'That's good news. How's the baby?'

'Taking the bottle quite happily since the lesson you gave her.'

Liv laughed and he couldn't help comparing her confidence at work with her lack of confidence in her social life.

'Have dinner with me tonight.' He'd spoken those words on umpteen occasions in the past, but never before had he braced himself for rejection. Up until this point in his life it had been a foregone conclusion that the woman in question would just say yes.

As he'd anticipated, Liv instantly shook her head. 'I couldn't possibly. Why? Why would you want to?'

He was asking himself the same question. He'd never before dated a colleague or a single mother.

Neither had he found himself thinking about sex at inconvenient moments during his working day. 'I owe you dessert.'

Liv backed towards the door. 'You don't owe me anything.'

Unaccustomed to having to persuade a woman to join him for dinner, Stefano watched her for a moment, trying to read her mind. 'Is it a babysitting issue?'

'Yes.' She said the word quickly and then breathed out and shook her head. 'No, actually that's not true. It isn't just about the babysitting. It's about *me*. And you. I mean, you found out everything there is to know about me last night. You've already listened to my entire life history and I'm sure it bored you to death. I don't have anything else to say. I work, I spend time with my child. That's it. I'm just not interesting. You already know all there is to know.'

He was stunned by the completely false impression she had of herself.

Why did she think she was boring?

Contemplating the soft curve of her mouth and the shyness in her expression, Stefano strolled across his office towards her. He watched as her eyes widened slightly.

'Mr Lucarelli—Stefano…'

Without speaking, Stefano took her face in his hands, stared down into her startled green eyes for a few endless seconds and then brought his mouth down on hers. For a moment she didn't move a muscle, and then she made a soft sound and her lips parted under his.

He kissed her slowly and confidently, taking his time, holding her head exactly as he wanted it as he skilfully seduced her mouth. Only when her fingers curled into the front of his shirt and he felt her relax against him did he slide an arm around her waist and pull her into his body.

Boring?

She was exquisite.

Her hips were curved, her breasts full and the sudden explosion of raw lust that devoured him was so powerful that it took all his willpower to stop himself from slamming the door shut and just taking her on his desk.

Unsettled by the fierce intensity of his own response, Stefano dragged his mouth from hers and eased her away from him.

Liv swayed for a moment and then opened her eyes and looked at him. Her expression was so bemused that he suddenly wondered exactly how long it had been since anyone had kissed her properly.

'There's plenty that I don't know about you, Liv,' he said softly, dragging his thumb over the swollen softness of her mouth. 'But I intend to find out.'

CHAPTER SIX

'MUMMY, why are you staring out of the window and smiling?'

Liv turned at the sound of Max's voice. 'Oh…' she cleared her throat and picked up her coffee-mug. It was Saturday morning and she'd been up since dawn. 'I was just…thinking.' *About being kissed*. It wasn't the first time she'd been kissed, but it seemed that way. Unless her memory was defective, it had never felt like that.

Stefano Lucarelli kissed as well as he did everything else.

Max shook the contents of the cereal packet into his bowl and looked at her sympathetically. 'Are you worrying that Father Christmas might not come? I know how he gets round the whole world in one night.'

'You do?' *Why had he kissed her?* She didn't understand it, but it was impossible to erase the memory from her brain or her body. And he'd said that he wanted to know more about her. *What had he meant by that?*

'Mum? Are you listening?'

'I'm listening.'

'It's because he travels through different time zones,' Max said seriously. 'You know, he starts in Australia, then he moves on to…' swinging his legs, he carried on detailing

Father Christmas's route while Liv tried desperately to stop thinking about Stefano.

With a huge effort, she brought herself back to reality. 'OK. I'll stop worrying about Father Christmas's workload. So—plan for the day. Football in the park and then we'll buy the Christmas tree. How does that sound?'

'Brilliant.' Max crunched his way through the cereal and drank his milk. 'Pizza for tea?'

Liv laughed. *Why was she feeling so happy?* It was completely ridiculous, but she just couldn't help it. Determined to pull herself together, she rose to her feet. 'I'll make the dough now. You can help. Wash your hands.'

'Hayley's mum won't let her make pizza dough because she says it makes a mess.' Max reached for the weighing scales and lifted the flour out of the cupboard. 'I told her that you love mess.'

'Mess and I are certainly intimately acquainted,' Liv said dryly, glancing around her kitchen and wondering why it never stayed tidy.

Because she was happy to let her son make pizza dough.

Max emptied some flour onto the weighing scales. 'Oops.' He stood back as some of it sprinkled over his toes. 'You can do the water.'

The doorbell rang just as Max plunged his fingers into the gooey mixture.

'That will be the postman.' Liv wiped her hands and walked towards the door. She was still in her pyjamas, her hair was tumbling loose past her shoulders and her feet were bare, but as she had no intention of stepping outside, she decided that it didn't matter.

Keeping her body out of sight, she opened the door, a cheerful smile on her face as she popped her head round.

Stefano Lucarelli stood there, a large white box in his hands and a cool, confident look on his handsome face. He was wearing a long black coat over jeans and a chunky roll-neck jumper that brushed against the blue shadow of his jaw.

'*Buongiorno.*'

Memories of that amazing kiss came flooding back with disturbing clarity and for a moment she wondered whether he was real or whether her mind had conjured him up because she'd been thinking of him all morning. *Was he a product of wishful thinking?*

'What are you doing here?' Liv winced as she listened to herself. It was no wonder she was single. 'I'm sorry. That sounded rude. It's just that I—' *He looked far too good to be standing in her doorway.*

'Invite me in.' His silken command left her more flustered than ever.

'You must be joking.' She thought of the pyjamas she was wearing. 'Why would you want to come in?'

'Because I don't want to eat dessert on my own.'

Her gaze shifted from the gleam in his eyes to the box in his hands. 'You brought me dessert?'

'Belgian chocolate log, complete with whipped cream.'

Liv started to laugh. 'It's ten o'clock in the morning.'

Stefano gave a dismissive shrug. 'If you're going to commit a sin, you may as well get it over with early in the day.' His Italian accent somehow made the words seem more sinful than the subject and the way he was looking at her made her insides turn to liquid.

'You can't possibly come in,' she said in a strangled voice. 'If you leave your Ferrari there, it will be gone when you leave. And anyway, I'm still in my pyjamas.'

'Are you? You probably shouldn't have told me that.' His

gaze focused on her for a moment. 'You have amazing hair. I had no idea it was so long.'

His words were so unexpected that everything she'd been about to say fizzled and died in her head. *He liked her hair?*

No, of course he didn't. How could he possibly? 'Now, you're being ridiculous,' she said gruffly. 'I look as though I just crawled out of bed.'

'Precisely.' His low, sexy drawl somehow connected to every nerve ending in her body.

Scarlet with embarrassment, she kept her body behind the door. 'I can't let you in.'

He smiled. 'Yes, you can.' He stepped forward and nudged at the door with his powerful shoulders.

'What are you doing?'

'Blasting you out of your comfort zone.' He strolled into her flat, pushed the door shut and scanned her body with a single glance. 'Nice pyjamas.' Amusement shimmered in his dark eyes. 'Pink baby elephants are absolutely my favourite animal.'

Aware that only a thin layer of cotton lay between his disturbingly thorough gaze and her naked body, Liv tried to cover herself and then realised the futility of the gesture and gave up. Why was life so unfair? When he'd taken her to dinner she'd been wearing her most ancient skinny rib jumper and now he'd arrived at her flat and she was dressed in cosy pyjamas that clung to her bottom and did nothing to hide the generous proportion of her top half.

Why couldn't she have been wearing a skimpy lacy number?

Because skimpy lacy numbers were designed for sex and seduction, not sleep.

She was about to make an excuse and vanish into her bedroom when Max emerged from the kitchen, trailing dough behind him.

'Did the postman bring something, Mum?'

'No.' Suddenly confronted by an issue far more serious than her choice of nightwear, Liv cleared her throat and tried to work out how best to explain the presence of a strange man in their hallway without upsetting Max.

She never brought men home.

But she didn't have to explain because Stefano took over. 'I work with your mother.' He dropped to his haunches and smiled at the child. 'Is that pizza dough you're wearing?'

Max grinned. 'It sort of just sticks everywhere.'

Stefano nodded with understanding. 'You could try using a little less water.'

Max considered that advice for a moment and then looked at Liv. 'You're adding too much water, Mum.'

Liv smiled weakly. 'That's probably where I'm going wrong.' She watched nervously as her son gave Stefano the once over.

'Are you staying for breakfast?' He peered at the box, his face brightening. 'What is that? Is it a present?'

'Max!'

But Stefano simply smiled and rose to his feet. 'It is a present. An edible present.' He handed the box to Liv. 'I heard that your mother likes dessert.'

Max was jumping up and down, sending pizza dough flying everywhere. 'She loves dessert but we don't often have it because she says it makes her fat. Can I see? Is it chocolate?'

Liv held the box in front of her like armour. 'I really need to get dressed,' she began, but Max was tugging her towards the kitchen.

'You look great, Mum,' he said earnestly. 'Why would you want to get changed? They're my favourite pyjamas. They're just so happy.'

Intercepting Stefano's laughing gaze, Liv closed her eyes.

Great.

The sexiest man alive was standing in her tiny hallway and she was wearing 'happy' pyjamas.

Why was he doing this? Why was he here?

Didn't he have anywhere better to be on a cold, sunny Saturday in December?

Max was giggling. 'This is *awesome*. Mum won't usually let me eat dessert unless I've finished my vegetables and I've never had dessert for breakfast before.'

They moved through to the tiny kitchen and Stefano instantly made himself at home, pulling out a chair and helping himself to a glass of orange juice.

Liv watched him out of the corner of her eye, wondering what he'd make of her tiny kitchen. But he didn't appear interested in anything other than Max.

'You need to cut the ribbon.' Picking up a knife, he leaned forward and sliced through the ribbon. The box fell open to reveal a beautiful chocolate log, dusted with icing and decorated with a snowman.

Max sank onto his chair, speechless. 'Wow. Have you seen it, Mum?'

'I've seen it, sweetheart.' And she didn't even want to imagine how many calories would be in a single slice.

'It's *amazing*.'

'I hope so.' Stefano picked up the knife. 'Would you like the piece from the end? There's more chocolate on that piece.' He sliced through the cake in a typically decisive fashion and Liv turned to put on the kettle, her mind working overtime.

Was he charming Max to get to her?

No, of course not. He wasn't interested in her. Why would he be interested in her?

But he *was* in her flat on his day off.

Her head was full of questions, but she didn't dare ask any of them while Max was there so she made a fresh pot of coffee and placed it in front of Stefano with an awkward smile. 'It isn't Italian. Cuban, I think.'

He leaned back in his chair and lifted an eyebrow. 'What happened to the instant?'

'Fresh coffee is my Saturday morning treat.' Liv raked her fingers through her long hair and then wished she hadn't because the gesture drew his gaze and she froze, sensing a shift in the mood and the atmosphere.

'We're going to play football in the park.' Aware that the adults were distracted, Max slid his hand towards the cake and transferred another piece onto his plate. 'Are you going to come?'

'Max!' Embarrassed and horrified, Liv dragged her gaze away from Stefano's and poured coffee into two mugs. 'Mr Lucarelli can't—I mean, he's very busy and he has to go in a minute and—'

'No, I don't. I'd love to play football.' Stefano stretched his long legs out in front of him and winked at the boy. 'As long as you are gentle with me. It's a long time since I played.'

'Do you like football?'

'I'm Italian,' Stefano pointed out. 'All Italians are born loving pizza, football and fast cars.'

'Perhaps I'm Italian.' For a moment Max forgot about the chocolate cake. 'Do you have a fast car?'

'Very fast.' Stefano smiled and Liv sat down opposite him, nursing her mug in her hands, watching as Max chatted.

'Cool. I'd love to drive it but I'm not old enough yet. I'm trying to make it into the first team at school. Mum's coaching me.'

'I'm not sure I'd exactly describe it as coaching.' Liv removed the remains of the chocolate log before Max was tempted to take a third slice. 'That was delicious. Thank you, Stefano.'

'Awesome.' Max watched wistfully as she put the cake away. 'Can we eat the rest later? After we've played football, we're going to buy our Christmas tree.'

Liv watched her son, her heart in her mouth. He was so, so trusting and while that was lovely in a way, it also terrified her. Despite not having a father, his little life had been stable and secure. She'd made sure of it. He didn't even remember Jack and he had no idea how much pain and anguish lurked out there in the world.

He had no idea what it felt like to be hurt.

Suddenly she felt a rush of protectiveness and for the first time since Stefano had knocked on her door, her voice was steady. 'Max, go and get changed. And spend ten minutes tidying your room.'

'But—'

'Untidy room, no football.'

With an exaggerated groan, Max slid off the chair and huffed his way out of the kitchen.

Liv closed the door behind him and Stefano's eyes narrowed.

'I sense I'm in trouble,' he said softly. 'Was it the chocolate log?'

'I need to know what you're doing here.' She stood with her back to the door, wishing she'd changed out of her pyjamas before she'd started this conversation. 'And don't tell me you were just bringing me dessert.'

'You refused my dinner invitation.'

'And you always bring breakfast round to women who refuse you?' When he didn't answer immediately, she gave a hollow laugh. 'Oh, don't tell me—no one has ever said no to you before. Is that what is going on here? Is it a pursuit thing? Is this about your ego, Stefano?'

He stirred. 'I don't have a problem with my ego.' He placed his mug back on the table in a deliberate movement. 'But I do enjoy your company.'

She thought about that comment for a moment and then let out a little breath and lifted a hand to her hair. 'Stefano, we both know that there are a million women out there who would give their entire salary to have breakfast with you. Women who are thinner and much more interesting than I am. So what I want to know is—what are you doing in my kitchen?'

'I heard a rumour that you wore pink elephant pyjamas.'

'Why are you joking?'

'Why are you so lacking in confidence?' His voice was soft. 'Why is it so unlikely that I would seek out your company?'

Liv looked at him in exasperation, aware that Max could emerge at any moment. 'Do I really have to spell it out?'

'Yes, I think you probably do.' Eyes narrowed, he watched her. 'I'd like to know what I'm dealing with.'

'You're dealing with someone ordinary, that's what you're dealing with. I try to be a good mother and I hope I'm a good nurse, but I'm not interesting and I'm *certainly* not sexy. I've had a *child*.' Listening to herself, she gave a groan and rolled her eyes to the ceiling. 'I cannot *believe* I'm having this conversation with you.'

'How could you possibly believe that you're not sexy?'

'Because I have a perfectly good mirror in my bedroom.' Liv forced herself to look him in the eye. 'I honestly don't know what you want from me. If it's sex, and I can't imagine for a moment that it would be,' she added hastily, 'then it's only fair to warn you that it's been so long since I did it, I'm not sure I can even remember how. I can guar-

antee that it would be the most crashing disappointment o
your life. Don't waste your time. I—I'm *ordinary*, Stefano.
The way he was looking at her made her hot and shivery a
the same time.

'If you don't think you're sexy then there is clearly some
thing wrong with your mirror.' His dark gaze lingered on he
face. 'And I don't find you in the least bit "ordinary". You ar
warm, kind, independent and unselfishly devoted to you
child. That makes you extraordinary, Liv, not ordinary.'

'Stefano—'

'I'm not here because you said no to me, I'm here becaus
I enjoy your company and I want to spend the day with you
Do I want to have sex with you?' He gave a slow smile and a
fatalistic lift of his broad shoulders. 'Yes, of course, I do. An
if you have forgotten how then don't worry, I will remind you.

'Stefano!'

'You're being honest, so I will be the same. I am Italia
and you are *extremely* sexy. But I'm willing to delay that par
until you feel a little more comfortable with me. Then we'l
see. Perhaps you will decide you'd like hot sex for Christma
after all.'

The colour poured into her cheeks and she closed her eyes
'So you *did* overhear our conversation.'

'Anna has a loud voice.'

'And she was voicing her own opinions, not mine,' Liv sai
in a strangled voice. 'I can't think of anything more horrify
ing than having hot sex with you—'

'Grazie.'

She covered her face with her hands. 'That didn't come ou
the way I meant it to come out. You must know how attractiv
you are—you don't need me to tell you that. It's just that—

'You're a nervous wreck,' he said, watching her with

faint hint of amusement in his lazy dark eyes. Unlike her, he was totally at ease with the conversation and with himself.

Her hands dropped to her sides and she gave a little shake of her head, knowing that whatever happened nothing would give her the courage to take her clothes off in front of this man.

'You don't want to go to a bed with a woman who eats chocolate log at ten in the morning.'

A slow, dangerous smile spread across his face. 'If you think that, *tesoro...*' he breathed gently '...then you truly know nothing about men. Being tempted by chocolate log in the morning, suggests a hedonistic, passionate nature and a real enjoyment of the good things in life. I look forward to uncovering more of this hidden side to you.'

The thought of him uncovering a single inch of her made her shrink with mortification, but at the same time her pulse was racing and her entire body was warm.

'Do you want to come and play football?' If there was one thing guaranteed to stop him looking at her in the way he was, it would be the sight of her shivering in goal with pink cheeks and blue lips.

He rose to his feet. 'Now that's an invitation I definitely can't refuse.'

It was the most entertaining day he'd had since his arrival in England.

The ground was hard and covered by frost, but Max sped down the field with the ball and kicked it into the goal. With whoops of joy he retrieved the ball and threw it to Stefano.

'Did you see me? Did you see me?' He was dancing on the spot with excitement and Stefano grinned.

'Great shot. But watch the position of your body,' he instructed, lining up the ball and demonstrating. 'Now you try.'

Max paused, distracted by two fire engines that raced along the nearby road, lights flashing, horns blaring. 'Wow,' he breathed, 'they're going so fast.'

Stefano glanced at them briefly and then took the opportunity to look at Liv.

She was standing in goal, occasionally shouting encouragement to her son. Her hands were in her pockets to keep them warm and she always seemed to move a few seconds after the ball had landed in the goal, but she was clearly doing her best.

And it was obvious that she hated football.

Stefano felt something shift inside him.

Offhand he couldn't think of a single other woman who would be prepared to spend an entire Saturday shivering, while a small boy kicked a ball into a net.

Yet she hadn't complained once, despite the fact that she was obviously freezing cold.

She'd changed out of her pyjamas into a thick wool sweater and a pair of jeans, but even with her wool coat and the addition of a thick scarf, he knew that she wasn't moving around enough to be able to stay warm. Her cheeks were pink, her lips were blue and suddenly he wanted to tackle her to the ground and warm her up in the most basic way known to man.

'Time for a break,' he called to both of them and together they strolled back towards the flat. Stefano was just wondering how to take the two of them out for lunch without triggering Liv's independent streak, when she gave a strangled cry.

'Oh no! Stefano, *no*! Those fire engines we saw—the fire is in our block of flats!'

Stefano turned his head and saw smoke and flames engulfing the building with horrifying speed. Two fire engines were parked outside and were tackling the blaze but even as they watched there was a small explosion and glass blew out of two upstairs windows.

With a horrified gasp, Liv started to run towards the flats and Stefano reached out and caught her arm in an iron grip. Her eyes still on her home, Liv tugged and tried to free herself but he closed his hands over her shoulders, holding her fast.

'No. You can't go in there. There's nothing you can do.' His tone was harsher than he'd intended but it seemed to have the desired effect because she stopped pulling and sagged against him.

'Our home. All our things...' Her voice was a helpless whisper and Max give a little sob and curled his fist into her coat for reassurance.

'Has our home gone, Mummy? Has it gone?'

'Oh, baby!' Forgetting her own anguish, she pulled away from Stefano and dropped to her knees, folding her son into her arms and squeezing him tightly. 'It's going to be fine, you'll see. It's just a little problem, but we can solve it together like we always do. Don't you worry.' Putting her own feelings to one side, she thought only of Max and Stefano watched in silence, at a loss to know what to say in the face of her personal disaster.

Remembering her reaction to the car, he knew how enormous this would be for her. But instead of falling apart and turning to him for support, she kept her emotions in check and concentrated on her child.

'Where will we live? Where will we sleep?' Max was crying now and he wrapped his arms round her neck and hung on tightly, clinging to his mother.

Stefano, who could never remember crying in his entire adult life, found that he had a lump in his throat.

'Hush. Hush now,' Liv said gently, 'that's enough. Stop

crying.' She eased him away from her and forced him to look at her. 'I'll fix it. You know I'll fix it.'

Even though everything she owned was in the building, currently being greedily devoured by flames, she held it together and the hand that stroked her son's head was remarkably steady.

Max's eyes swam. 'My toys are in there,' he choked, 'and my special moon and stars bed cover and my geography colouring.'

Stefano watched as Liv somehow conjured up a magical smile full of confidence and reassurance. 'Well, I'm willing to bet that Mr Thompson hasn't heard *that* excuse before for not handing in homework on time. I think he just might forgive you, this once.' Her tone was light and she leaned forward and kissed Max several times. 'It's people that matter, sweetheart, not things. Remember that. Things aren't important. They can always be replaced. We have each other, and that's all that really matters.' But although her words were brave and seemed to reassure Max, her face was as white as a winter frost and her eyes were blank with shock.

He needed to get both of them away from here.

Stefano was about to take charge when she straightened, still holding Max's hand.

'There's no point in standing here watching.' Her voice was steady and strong. 'It's upsetting for Max. There's a coffee-shop round the corner. I'll take him there while I ring the insurance company and work out what to do. They're going to have to arrange for us to stay somewhere tonight.'

A flicker of movement in the flats caught Stefano's eye. 'Liv—there's someone up there. One flat below yours.'

Still holding tightly to Max's hand, Liv followed the direction of his gaze. 'It's Emma,' she breathed in horror. 'She's eleven. Where's her mother? Why are they still in there?'

'She needs to get down on the floor,' Max muttered, pressing himself against Liv's leg. 'We were taught that in school. Smoke rises, so you need to get down on the floor.'

Stefano glanced at Liv. He didn't want to leave her, but she clearly read his mind because she gave him a push.

'We're fine. Go. Be careful.'

'Stay here,' Stefano ordered. 'Call an ambulance, Liv. At the very least she's going to suffer from smoke inhalation.'

By the time he'd identified himself to the crew, two firemen in breathing apparatus had appeared from the building carrying the child.

Swiftly Stefano carried out an initial assessment. 'Do we have any idea of the nature of the materials in her flat? Furniture, polyurethane foam?'

Liv appeared by his side, as cool and composed as she always was in a medical crisis. There was nothing to indicate that her own home had been one of those destroyed. 'Emma?' She stroked the child's hair gently. 'It's Liv, from upstairs—how are you feeling, sweetheart?'

'I didn't hear anything,' the little girl said hoarsely and then gave a choking cough. 'I was asleep.' She made a whistling sound as she inhaled and Stefano saw Liv glance at him.

'She has a degree of stridor. Do you want to intubate her?'

'I want to give her oxygen and get her to hospital. If I have to intubate her, I will, but this obviously isn't the best place.' Stefano cursed mentally, aware that Liv's home was burning behind him and he was going to have to make a difficult choice. The shriek of an ambulance siren announced the arrival of the paramedics.

'Max and I will follow in the car,' Liv said immediately. 'We might be able to help and at least we'll be able to give you a lift back here.'

Stefano thrust a hand in his pocket and withdrew his keys. 'Use my car.'

'You're joking.' Her expression was comical. 'I can't drive a Ferrari. I'll take the hire car and we can collect yours later.'

At that moment there was a piercing scream and a woman dropped her shopping and ran towards them. Food spilled over the pavement and a milk carton split and slowly leaked its contents into the gutter. 'Emma!' The woman stared at the stretcher and then put her hands to her mouth. 'Oh my God— is she? Is she—?'

About to transfer the child to the ambulance, Stefano cast a meaningful look in Liv's direction. She slid her arm round the woman, supporting and restraining her so that she didn't obstruct the transfer of her daughter into the ambulance.

'Emma's all right, Susan. But she's breathed in some of the smoke so we need to take her to the hospital. You can follow in the car with us.'

Susan looked over her shoulder at the smouldering building. 'Our home…'

'Let's worry about Emma first.' Liv didn't even glance towards her flat, but Susan started to sob.

'I've lost everything. Everything. All my Christmas presents were in there and I certainly can't afford to buy another lot.'

Stefano gritted his teeth. Her daughter was lying on a stretcher and she was worrying about her Christmas presents? Deciding that he would never cease to be disgusted by the shallowness of human nature, he climbed into the ambulance, wishing that he didn't have to leave Liv.

Just before the doors closed, he glanced back at her and saw her speaking reassuringly to Susan, while cuddling Max.

She supported everyone, he thought grimly. *But who supported her?*

CHAPTER SEVEN

THEY decided to admit Emma, and Liv was helping Susan make a call to the insurance company when Stefano strode into the room.

'Liv?'

Relieved to see him, she gently extracted herself from Susan's clutches. 'Go and see Emma.' Checking that Susan had everything she needed, Liv followed him out of the room. 'She's terribly upset.'

'I noticed. More upset about her things than her daughter,' he said in a cool tone.

'It's hard for her. Her husband left in the summer and she's been really struggling.' Liv ran her fingers over her forehead, trying to ease the throbbing ache. 'Anyway, Emma will be fine and that's the main thing. Are you going home now?' Just saying the word made her feel slightly strange because she realised that she didn't have a home to go back to. 'I need to talk to the fire service.'

'I've just done it. The blaze is out but it's too soon for them to assess the damage. They think it was caused by faulty Christmas-tree lights in a flat on the ground floor.' He frowned. 'You look awful. You need to rest. You and Max can stay with me for now.'

Liv was so stunned by his unexpected offer that for a moment she just gaped at him. Then she shook her head. 'No way. We couldn't possibly.'

'I'm not letting you refuse, so don't even waste time arguing.' His tone was forceful but she still hesitated.

'That's far too generous an offer. I just…couldn't.'

'Yes, you could. And you will.'

'Having me around will cramp your style.'

'What style is that?' His eyes gleamed with irony. 'Liv, you've seen my life. I work. When I get home, I sleep. You won't be cramping anything. I want you to move in.'

She couldn't believe he was making this offer. 'You've never let a woman move in with you.'

'That's because I don't like anyone tracking my movements. And I hate anyone asking what time I'm finishing work. You won't do that because the chances are that you'll be stuck at work, too. Now stop arguing and just say yes.'

It was such an overwhelming gesture that she felt her throat close. 'Max is a very lively little boy,' she said thickly. 'He'll break something. They say that trouble comes in threes. My car is dead, my flat is no more—perhaps the third thing will be Max breaking something valuable that I can't afford to replace.'

'He can break anything he likes. It's a home, not a museum.' Visibly exasperated, Stefano raked his fingers through his hair. 'Liv, for once just say yes.'

'Why?' She looked at him helplessly. 'Why are you doing this?'

'Because I like you.'

'You…do? You like me?' Her car was dying, her house had just burned down. But the way Stefano was looking at her made her feel as though something amazing had just happened.

'I like you.' A muscle flickered in his jaw. 'And I like Max.'

Overwhelmed, she took a step backwards. 'Don't do that,' she said hoarsely. 'Don't be nice to me, Stefano, or I'll bawl all over you again and you know how much you enjoyed it the last time.'

'I'm not giving you sympathy. I'm giving you a solution to your problems. Take it.' He paused as a nurse hurrying past shot them a curious look. 'Liv, Max is still waiting in my office. He's upset and worried. He needs to know where he is sleeping tonight and he doesn't need some anonymous hotel room. Go and talk to him. Explain that we're going to buy his Christmas tree. We can sort out where you're going to live permanently when Christmas is over.' Stefano pulled his phone out of his pocket. 'You fetch Max and meet me by the car. I'll do the rest.'

Stefano's apartment was in an exclusive red-brick building overlooking the wide expanse of Hyde Park.

Feeling as though she was living someone else's life, Liv held tightly to Max's hand as Stefano negotiated the tight security that formed an apparently impenetrable cordon at the base of the building.

Still shocked by everything that had happened, Max barely spoke until they were through the glass doors.

Then his youthful curiosity gradually reasserted itself. 'Wow, that scanner thing is amazing,' he breathed as Stefano gently urged them across the gleaming marble floor towards the lift. 'Like something out of a spy movie.'

'I smell of smoke.' Liv wrinkled her nose in distaste and Stefano flicked some debris from his long coat.

'It clings, doesn't it? As soon as we get upstairs, you can take a bath.'

And then what? She didn't have any clothes to change into but Liv didn't say anything. Presumably the insurance would eventually cover most of what they'd lost, but in the short term it was going to cost her a fortune.

A fortune that she didn't have.

Perhaps she would have to work Christmas Day after all, she thought miserably. *Just for the money.*

Suddenly it all seemed like too much.

She'd been holding it together for Max, but the sheer size of the problem she was facing made her want to curl into a ball and give up.

How was she going to cope?

The lift purred soundlessly upwards and when the doors finally opened Liv gave a gasp.

Max spoke first. 'Which bit is your house?' He spoke in a soft, awed voice and Stefano smiled and took his hand.

'All of it. It's not a house, it's an apartment. I own the whole of this floor. Come on, I'll show you your bedroom.'

'All of it? All of this is yours?' Max tilted his head back and stared up at the endless glass and spacious elegance. 'It's bigger than the hospital.'

Stefano picked him up and lifted him onto his shoulders. 'There—now it doesn't seem so big.'

'Wow, this is terrific!' Max whooped with excitement and dug his fingers into Stefano's hair. Liv winced but part of her was overwhelmed with gratitude because he'd made her little boy smile.

With her son on his shoulders, his bronzed hands holding the child steady, Stefano seemed nothing like the intimidating consultant she worked with in the emergency department.

'I'll show you the bedroom I think you'll like, but you can choose a different one if you prefer.' He strode across the pale wooden floor, opened a door and lifted the boy off his shoulders in an easy movement. 'What do you think?'

'It's like mine,' Max said in wonder. 'Only bigger. It's a space capsule, Mum.'

'Yes. Aren't you lucky?'

'I have twin nephews the same age as Max.' Stefano strolled across to the window. 'They chose the décor.'

'They like the same things as me.' Max clambered onto the cabin bed and vanished under a canopy of moons and stars. 'This is so cool. It's just like being at home only better.' His little head peeped round the side of the canopy. 'Is it OK to say that Mum? That doesn't make you sad, does it?'

'You never make me sad,' Liv said quickly. 'I'm pleased you like it. It's very kind of Stefano to have us.'

Stefano steered her out of the bedroom and back into the glorious living room that overlooked the park.

Beneath them she could see horses cantering sedately along a track, their breath forming clouds in the freezing air. Mothers wrapped up in scarves and long elegant coats pushed buggies and watched toddlers romping in the snow.

'It's a fabulous place.'

'You make it sound like a problem.'

She gave a wry smile, her eyes still on the view. 'I'm hoping that it won't be too much of a wrench for Max to go back to his real life after this.'

'Don't think about that and anyway, you're his real life. You're his security. As long as *you're* all right, so is he.' Stefano put his hands on her shoulders and turned her towards him, a frown in his eyes as he studied her face. 'You're exhausted. Can you stop thinking and worrying for just five minutes and let me sort things out? Max and I are going to buy a Christmas tree and you are going to lie in a hot bubble bath for an hour.'

'An hour?' She was horribly aware of him, her heart thudding in a crazy rhythm against her chest. 'I wouldn't know what to do in a bath for an hour.'

'That's the point.' Amusement gleamed in his eyes. 'You do nothing.' He gave a slow smile and then his gaze slid to her mouth and lingered.

'Mum?'

Liv jumped backwards. 'Yes?' Flustered, she licked her lips, as if Stefano's gaze had left a mark she had to remove. 'You're going to buy a Christmas tree. Don't buy a big one.' Reaching for her bag, she pulled out her purse. 'This is our budget. Don't argue.' She stuffed the money into Stefano's hand. 'Thank you.'

For a moment he didn't respond. He simply looked at the money in his hand and then glanced at her face. Then he smiled and slid the money into a soft billfold, as if he knew that to refuse would make her uncomfortable.

'*Grazie*. Now go and relax and leave everything to us boys.'

'Do you like that one?' Stefano watched as Max gazed at the huge, glittering Christmas tree in the window of the exclusive Knightsbridge store.

'It's amazing,' Max breathed, his head tilted backwards as he scanned it all the way to the top. 'Like something out of a Christmas movie.'

'Good.' Wishing all decisions were as easy, Stefano strode through the doors and into the store, Max by his side.

Within seconds he found an assistant, briefed her on what he wanted and then looked down at Max who was tugging at his sleeve. 'What's the matter? You've decided that you want a different one?'

'No, but—you can't buy the one in the window,' Max whispered. 'It isn't for sale.'

Stefano smiled. 'It is now.'

'Really?' Max glanced over his shoulder, as if checking that his imagination hadn't been playing tricks. 'What about the decorations?'

'Those too.'

'But what about the decorations you already have at home? Aren't you going to use those?'

'I don't have any decorations at home.'

Max looked startled. 'But what do you usually put on your tree?'

'Nothing.' Stefano handed his credit card to the assistant. 'I don't usually have a tree.'

'*You don't have a tree?*' Max looked shocked. 'Not even a small one?'

'No.'

'Why not?'

'I don't bother with a tree because I usually spend Christmas on my own.'

There was a long silence while Max digested that fact. 'That's terrible,' he said in a hushed voice. 'Mum told me that some people are on their own for Christmas and that's just the *worst* thing.' His expression sympathetic, he slid his arms round Stefano and gave him a hug. 'Well, this year you won't have to be lonely,' he said solemnly, 'because *we're* going to keep you company. We can stay as long as you need us.'

Oblivious to the team of sales assistants who were casting him covetous glances as they busily collated the decorations for the tree, Stefano stood still, too stunned by the child's warmth and generosity to answer immediately. Then he put his hand on the boy's shoulder and squeezed gently. '*Grazie*,' he said softly, '*thank you*.' The child was like his mother. *Always thinking about other people*.

'You're welcome. Mum always makes Christmas amazing.' Max's eyes widened as the assistant wrapped the boxes of decorations. 'I hope it isn't costing too much,' he whispered. 'It can't cost too much or Mum will just worry.'

'Does she worry a lot?'

'All the time. She thinks she's hiding it but I just *know*.' The child glanced up. 'Girls don't always say what they mean, do they?'

Stefano hid a smile. 'No,' he said wryly. 'They certainly don't.'

'It's weird really,' Max said frankly. 'I mean, if I'm worried about something I just say it straight out. Mum tries to hide it. Why does she do that?'

'I expect she doesn't want to worry you.'

'But I always know when she's worried because she has a different face. Her smile is bigger when she's really worried, like she's trying extra hard to hide the fact that she's worried. And when it's money that's worrying her she makes lots of lists and does a lot of adding up. Just to check she doesn't run out. But if something new comes along she has to cross something out.'

Stefano digested that information for a moment. 'So what do you think she'd like for Christmas?'

'Oh that's easy.' Max looked smug. 'A hug.'

'A *hug*?'

'Yes.' Max picked up a frosted bauble from the display and examined it closely. 'Whenever you ask Mum what she wants for Christmas, she always says "a really big hug". Which is a bit weird, to be honest. I mean, I love anything with a remote control, but she's just happy with cuddles. Girls are pretty easy to please, aren't they?'

Never having encountered a girl who was easy to please, Stefano gave a sardonic smile. 'Your mother is easy to please.'

The assistant cleared her throat and returned his credit card. 'Could you give me a delivery address, sir?'

'We haven't finished shopping yet.' Making an instantaneous decision, Stefano took Max's hand. 'Come on. We need to replace some of the things you lost.'

Max hung back. 'Where's the money coming from? Did Mum sell her tickets to the ball or something?'

Tucking his credit card back into his wallet, Stefano looked at the child. 'She had tickets to a ball? The hospital ball?'

'Yes, she won them. But she doesn't want them so she's going to sell them to someone who can go. She can't go because she's not Cinderella.'

Stefano exhaled slowly and squatted down next to the little boy. 'Did she tell you that?'

'Yes. She said it the morning the tickets arrived in the post.' Max shrugged. 'She sort of looked at them in a funny way, said that she'd never won anything in her life before, and then put them back in the envelope. Then she said something like "I'm not Cinderella and I'm not going to a ball." But she hasn't given them away. They're in her handbag. I saw them when she gave me my pocket money.'

Stefano digested that information and then straightened, 'I don't know about you, Max,' he said idly, 'but it seems a terrible waste not to use those tickets.'

'She doesn't want to go because she thinks her bottom is too big and she doesn't have anything to wear. Girls really care about things like that,' Max said sagely and Stefano smiled.

'Then we'd better fix that, hadn't we? Are you any good at keeping secrets?'

Hearing laughter and Max's excited chatter, Liv emerged from the bathroom self-consciously, wrapped in a large soft robe that Stefano had given her.

'Mum, Mum come and see this tree!' Max was almost exploding with excitement and he darted across Stefano's apartment as if it had been his home all his life. 'We're going to decorate it together.'

'You bought decorations?' Eyeing the size of the tree and then the number of parcels and bags that now littered the floor of the room, Liv felt a flutter of panic.

Max immediately hurled himself across the room and hugged her. 'You're not to worry. Stefano needed a tree anyway and he needed decorations.' He lowered his voice. 'He didn't have any. Can you believe that?'

Liv glanced towards Stefano and he gave a wicked little smile.

'Nice bath?'

Suddenly conscious that she was naked under the robe, she blushed. 'Lovely. Thank you.'

'I bought you some clothes. Just some basic stuff to tide you over until you can go shopping yourself.' He handed her several bags, as if it were nothing. 'I hope they fit.'

Liv's stomach lurched as she stared at the label on the bags. 'You didn't—'

'You can't spend the next few weeks dressed in a bathrobe.' Stefano's eyes gleamed dangerously and then he turned back to Max and took the box of lights from him. 'Where do you want these?'

How could she argue when she needed something to wear? Resolving to find some way of paying him back, Liv picked up the bags. 'Thank you.'

She retreated to the beautiful bedroom and delved into the bags. Jeans? Her heart sank and she dropped them onto the bed. *Why did it have to be jeans?* This was going to be so *unbelievably* embarrassing. She could never find jeans to fit so there was no way he was going to have succeeded. The thought of confessing that she was actually three sizes larger than his estimate, made her shrink with embarrassment.

Postponing the moment when she had to try and pull them over her thighs, she delved into the bag again and hot colour flooded into her cheeks as she pulled out the pretty silk and lace bra. This was getting worse by the minute. How could she wear that? She needed something far more robust. Stefano had never seen her in anything that wasn't baggy, so obviously he wasn't going to have a clue what size—

Her thoughts tangled as she looked at the label. The bra was exactly the right size and she dropped it as if it were scalding hot.

How had he known what size to buy?

Horribly self-conscious, she turned and stared at the closed door, half expecting him to be watching her with that sexy smile on his face.

She couldn't even tell herself that it was because he was very, very experienced with women, because she didn't think for a moment that he would have had any experience with women of *her* size.

Pulling on the silk panties, she was momentarily sidetracked by the fact they felt so decadently luxurious against her skin. Then she tried the bra and was amazed to find that it not only felt secure, it looked fabulous.

He had excellent taste in underwear, she thought weakly, reaching for the jeans.

Braced for humiliation she pulled them up, but instead of becoming stuck on her thighs as she'd expected, they slid over her legs, moulded to her bottom and fastened easily.

Unable to believe he'd bought her a perfect pair of jeans when she'd never succeeded in doing that, Liv glanced at the label and then wished she hadn't because she knew instantly that they'd cost him a fortune.

She knew she ought to tell him to take them back. But then she glanced at herself in the mirror and they looked so impossibly good that she almost giggled with delight.

Her legs looked long and slender, her bottom curvy and—

Eyeing her cleavage, she sighed.

She needed a top.

Opening another bag, she found a luxuriously soft cashmere jumper in a shade of green that she loved, together with a scarf, a hat and an adorable pair of gloves.

Feeling like someone completely different, she strolled out into the living room.

'What is this? Make-over time?'

'No, those are the basics.' Stefano was reaching up to place a bauble at the top of the tree. 'A make-over is something entirely different. Do they fit? It was a bit of a rushed selection. Max and I didn't have much time.' He turned to look at her and his eyes swept over her in blatant masculine appraisal

'These jeans are amazing.' Disconcerted by the look in his eyes, she looked down at herself. 'It's like having plastic surgery.'

'You don't need plastic surgery.' His tone exasperated, h

strolled towards her and took her face in his hands. 'You're gorgeous, Liv.'

Her eyes slid towards Max and Stefano exhaled slowly and let his hands drop to his sides. 'I'm glad everything fits.'

'I don't even want to know how you knew my size,' she muttered and he gave a knowing smile.

'Guesswork.' The way he was looking at her made her feel dizzy and breathless and the clothes made her feel—well, they made her feel *incredible*.

'Thank you.'

'It's a pleasure.' His gaze lingered on hers for a moment and then he turned his attention back to the tree.

But there was a tension in his broad shoulders that hadn't been there before and Liv felt a sudden rush of exhilaration because she knew that there was chemistry between them. She didn't understand it, but it was definitely there.

The question was, would she dare to do anything about it?

By the middle of December the whole hospital was buzzing with excitement at the prospect of the Snowflake Ball. Those without tickets were hoping desperately for a sudden flurry of returns and those with tickets spent the day of the ball discussing how to look glamorous and stay warm at the same time.

'Everyone has gone mad,' Liv grumbled as she handed Anna a pile of notes. 'It's just a dance. With all the same people they work with every day.'

'In case you hadn't noticed, a dinner jacket is so much more attractive than a scrub suit.'

'But once you've seen them in a scrub suit, there's no going back.' Liv said dryly. 'I'm glad I gave my tickets to you. What are you wearing?'

'Oh!' Anna avoided her gaze. 'I haven't decided yet.'

Liv looked at her in amazement. 'But it's tonight.'

'I know. But we finish at four. That gives me four hours to decide what to wear. That should just about be enough.'

'You should have let me have Sam for the night.'

'You don't think that two little boys in Stefano's flashy apartment would have been pushing things?' Anna smiled. 'Anyway, there's no need. Dave's mother has turned up for her annual Christmas take-over, so she might as well make herself useful. How's Max doing? Is he sleeping in his own bed yet?'

'Yes. He only slept with me for the first couple of nights. He seems to be fine, actually. And that's because of Stefano. Max is so cocooned in this wonderful masculine world of football and Ferraris that I think he's forgotten that his own home no longer exists.'

'Sam told me all about Stefano turning up at school in the Ferrari to collect Max.'

'Yes. That was probably the highlight of Max's life so far.'

Anna looked at her closely. 'And you're not happy about that?'

Liv bit her lip. 'I'm happy that he's happy, of course I am. But I'm also worried about what is going to happen in the new year. At the moment Max is living in style. He's made friends with the whole of the security team in Stefano's apartment block and they play spy games with him all the time. He goes for rides in Stefano's Ferrari. How is he going to adapt to returning to his own life?'

'He's just having fun. You're the reality of his life, Liv. You're the anchor. But that doesn't mean he can't have fun while it's on offer.' Anna touched her shoulder. 'And you should do the same. Just enjoy it while it's there. Life is a cold, hard thing as you well know. If there's any warmth available, then take it and make the most of it.'

'That's what I'm doing.' Liv thought of her new clothes and Stefano's incredible apartment. 'He has this balcony that wraps itself around the whole apartment. It's fabulous. And it's so, so peaceful.' She took a deep breath. 'And it feels safe. In the flat I always slept with one eye open in case someone tried to break in and there were often fights on the streets outside. Living in Knightsbridge is like moving to a different country.'

'All right, I've heard enough.' Laughing, Anna covered her ears with her hands. 'Any moment now I'm going to thump you. Just don't tell me that you've seen Stefano naked. That will *really* ruin my day.'

'One of the advantages of an extremely large apartment is that it's perfectly possible for two people not to see that much of each other.'

And that was a good thing, she told herself firmly. He'd been so generous that she was starting to imagine things she shouldn't imagine.

Yes, he'd said that he wanted to have sex with her, but he was a man, wasn't he? And she had no doubt at all that if Stefano ever caught a glimpse of her without the clothes he'd bought, he'd change his mind about finding her attractive.

Anna peered at her closely. 'Is something going on I should know about?'

Liv felt her heart bump. 'Nothing.' She wasn't going to mention that one incredible kiss in his office because since then he hadn't laid a finger on her so obviously he'd changed his mind about finding her attractive.

'Well you've been living with him for over a week so if there's nothing going on then you're a disgrace to the female race. You're living with the sexiest man alive. If you haven't used the opportunity to seduce him, you should be ashamed of yourself.'

Liv picked up another set of notes and went to call the patient. 'Seduction usually involves undressing. And I don't do undressing unless I'm by myself or I'm in the dark.'

Anna slid into Stefano's office. 'This is never going to work. You're never going to get her into a balldress and you're never going to persuade her to relax enough to dance with you.'

'That is my problem.' Stefano put his pen down. 'Is everything else arranged?'

'Yes, yes.' Anna paced nervously across the room. 'But she has *no* confidence, you know that, don't you?'

Yes, he knew that.

Accustomed to women who were tediously preoccupied with their own appearance, he was finding Liv a revelation. 'Stop worrying.'

Anna shot him a look. 'The suspense is killing me.' She folded her arms. 'I don't think I've actually ever kept a secret before. And how on earth has Max managed not to let it all spill out? Sam is the same age and he can't keep a secret if you pay him.'

'It helps to own a Ferrari,' Stefano said dryly and Anna laughed.

'You're bribing him with your car? You Italians have no sense of decency.'

'Max wants her to go to the ball. You're sure you haven't changed your mind?'

'About giving you the tickets? Of course not. But I'm not convinced this whole thing is going to work. Thanks to her delightful ex-husband, Liv doesn't think she's beautiful and no amount of Cinderella treatment is going to change that. Why are you smiling?'

'Because by the time I have finished,' Stefano murmured,

'Liv will *know* she's beautiful.' *It was going to give him enormous pleasure to take care of that. Personally.*

'Oh for heaven's sake.' Anna fanned herself and sank into the nearest chair. 'Just don't break her heart, Stefano, or I'll chop you into pieces. Do you need any advice? Her favourite colour? Best shoes to make a woman gasp? What to say to turn a woman to mush? No.' She chuckled and shook her head. 'You don't need any advice on women at all, do you, you sexy beast.'

'I think I can struggle through.' Amused, Stefano checked his watch. 'You won't forget to pick Max up from school?'

'Of course not.' Anna stood up again and paced the floor. 'Will you phone me with an interim report?'

'No. I intend to be fully occupied.'

Anna's own smile faded. 'Why are you doing this? Is it just about sex?'

'Would it matter if it was?' Stefano watched her closely. She was Liv's best friend. She knew her better than anyone. 'Incredibly good sex can make a woman feel beautiful, too.'

'Just as long as she isn't dumped immediately afterwards,' Anna muttered. 'I suppose I just feel responsible. I agreed to go along with all this because it sounds pretty romantic to me, but if it's all going to end in—'

'Anna,' Stefano interrupted her gently. 'It's half past three.'

'Yes, yes. I'm going to pick the kids up now. Just make sure you live up to your reputation, Mr Lucarelli.'

'You believe what you read in newspapers?'

'In this case, I want to.' Anna glared at him. 'I want you to be as good as that disgustingly skinny ex-girlfriend of yours says you are, or Father Christmas just might do something unspeakable to your Ferrari.'

CHAPTER EIGHT

Liv changed slowly, lifted her bag from the locker and smiled at a couple of her colleagues who were buzzing with excitement and on their way to the hairdresser's in preparation for the ball.

She was going to have a lovely evening with Max.

They'd make pizza. Maybe they could curl up and watch a film in Stefano's den. It had deep squashy sofas and a huge cinema screen and it was definitely Max's favourite room.

She wasn't going to think about the fact that Stefano hadn't made a single move towards her since she'd moved into his apartment. Of course he hadn't. That kiss had just been a— Well she didn't exactly know what it was, but it certainly hadn't meant anything.

She left the hospital and walked across the car park. And then stopped as she saw Stefano. He was leaning against the Ferrari, his arms folded, obviously waiting for her.

He looked so spectacularly handsome that for a moment her mind just emptied and then she remembered that he wasn't supposed to be here.

Anxiety rushed over her. 'I thought you were picking Max up.'

'Slight change in the arrangements.' He opened the car door. 'Get in.'

'But—'

'Max is safe.' He slid into the driver's seat next to her. 'He's gone to Anna's for the night. And for the next twelve hours at least I don't want you to argue with me or question me. I just want you to say "*Sì*, Stefano."'

Bemused, Liv just looked at him, a hundred questions bubbling round in her head. 'That isn't fair. I need to know—'

'Do you trust me?' His voice was deep and velvety smooth and she felt her mouth dry.

'Yes. No.' Her eyes met his. 'I trust you with my son. I think.'

He smiled. 'That's good enough.' The Ferrari gave a throaty growl and several heads turned towards them as he drove out of the car park.

'Am I allowed to ask where we're going?'

'No.'

'Am I allowed to talk to Max?'

He glanced towards her. 'Would it make you feel better if you did?'

'I just need to know he's happy.'

'Then call.'

'He's at Anna's?'

'They might have gone for a treat. Call Anna's mobile.'

'But she'll be getting ready for the ball.' Wishing she knew what was going on, Liv dialled and spoke to Anna who immediately passed the phone to Max.

Liv hung up feeling better, but none the wiser. 'Why did he say "have a nice evening"?'

'Probably because he wants you to have a nice evening.' Stefano pulled up outside a top London hotel.

A uniformed man immediately stepped forward and opened the door. 'Miss Winchester? We've been expecting you.'

They had? Liv glanced at Stefano but he simply smiled.

'I'll pick you up in three hours. Enjoy.'

Enjoy what? What was she going to do for three hours?

'What's this all about? Please tell me.'

Stefano took her face in his hands and lowered his head so that his mouth was almost touching hers. Almost, but not quite. 'The next three hours are about *you*, Liv,' he said softly. 'And after that, it's about *us*. Lie there and think about that while you're being pampered.'

Pampered?

The questions flew from her brain as his mouth brushed hers in a seductive, deliberate kiss designed to tantalise rather than provide satisfaction.

Liv's head swam dizzily as he slowly lifted his mouth from hers and smiled.

'Enjoy yourself. Think about nothing but yourself. Promise?'

How could one kiss cause so much havoc?

Trying to control the fireworks in her insides, Liv allowed herself to be led through the elegant hotel lobby. Feeling like the only person in the world who wasn't in on a secret, she followed the man into a lift, which slid soundlessly upwards to the top floor of the hotel. The doors opened onto a tranquil, luxurious spa overlooking the rooftops of London.

Stunned, Liv glanced around her at the acres of cool marble, glass and mirrors. 'What is this place?'

'I believe that most women believe it to be the place closest to heaven, madam,' the man said dryly, guiding her towards an immaculately groomed woman in a white uniform. 'This is Irina. She will take very good care of you.'

The next three hours passed in a blur of scented oils and relaxation. Liv was taken into a softly lit room filled with the exotic flowers and the relaxing sounds of tiny, bubbling fountains. Having changed into a soft white robe, she was given a massage that almost sent her to sleep.

'I've never had one of these before,' she murmured, 'but it's heaven. I don't want it to end.'

Irina covered her with a warm towel. 'Unfortunately it has to be a little shorter than usual because we still need to do your nails, hair and make-up. We don't have much time.'

Liv lifted her head. 'Before what?'

The girl smiled. 'Before Stefano Lucarelli picks you up. The car will be here just before eight. And we want you to look your best.'

'I have no idea what is going on, and I don't even care any more,' Liv murmured, closing her eyes again. 'The only downside is realising what I've been missing all these years. I'm not sure I'm going to be able to get through the rest of my life without a massage a day.'

Glancing at his watch, Stefano strode through the doors of the hotel and into the foyer.

They were cutting it fine, but hopefully the traffic would be in their favour.

Unless she was late.

Simmering with impatience because he'd given the staff of the spa a *very* precise brief, Stefano lifted his phone out of his pocket and was just about to blast someone into outer space when he saw her.

Her silver gown shimmered and sparkled under the lights. It fell from her neck to the floor, skimming her incredible curves and displaying just enough cleavage to ensure that none of the men in the hotel were able to continue a conversation. Her hair had been swept up in a style that was both elegant and contemporary and was held in place by a single white gold and diamond snowflake.

Stefano gave a satisfied smile. The white gold and diamond snowflake that *he'd* chosen. Matching diamond snowflakes dangled from her ears, sparkling against the slender column of her throat.

The only colour was the vivid red of her scarlet mouth and the green of her eyes, which were looking at him with a mixture of excitement and nerves.

Mentally congratulating himself, Stefano strode across to her and lifted her hand to his lips. 'You look stunning.'

Her eyes were on his, anxious, seeking reassurance. 'Really?'

'Do you need proof?' He slid his other arm round her waist and pulled her against him. 'I'm beginning to wish we weren't going out.' His eyes drifted to the tempting shadow of her cleavage. The way he was feeling, he just wanted to check into the nearest room and rip the silver dress from her delicious body.

'I'm presuming we're going to the ball?'

Her excitement was infectious and he smiled. 'What makes you think that?'

'I don't suppose you went to all this trouble to take me for a bowl of spaghetti at Luigi's,' she joked, 'and given that Anna currently has my child, and I'm wearing an amazing dress— Did you choose the dress?'

'I gave them the jewellery and a brief.' A brief to make sure that she looked sexy, glamorous and incredibly feminine.

They'd excelled themselves, he decided, dragging his gaze from her lips and scanning her body.

'This dress is amazing and the diamonds…' She lifted her fingers to the snowflakes dangling from her ears. 'I'm scared to wear them. What if I lose them?'

'They're yours to lose or to keep.' Stefano shrugged. 'Enjoy them.' Knowing how fiercely independent she was, he braced himself for an argument, but she gave him a delicious smile that increased the heat in his groin by a thousand degrees.

'I *know* I ought to argue with you and insist on giving them back,' she confided, 'but I can't. I love them too much. Does that make me greedy?'

'No, it makes you a woman.' A gorgeous, captivating sexy woman. 'It also makes me pleased. It's always nice to know that a gift is well received.' Engulfed by an explosion of raw, savage lust, Stefano was starting to wish he'd arranged for a private dinner instead of a very public, glittering Christmas ball.

'I *feel* like a woman. I feel...*fabulous*. The dress is just amazing and I'm never going to take it off.'

She glowed like a candle and he couldn't take his eyes from her face.

'I will be the one taking it off, *tesoro*,' Stefano murmured huskily and watched with satisfaction as her pupils dilated and her lips parted. Soft colour touched her cheeks and the fact that she couldn't hide the way she felt about him simply intensified the almost agonising ache in his groin.

'Stefano.' she sounded breathless. 'I honestly— It's been such a long time—'

He covered her mouth with the tips of his fingers. 'Anything you have forgotten, I will remind you.' Seriously aroused, Stefano dragged his eyes from her lush, quivering body and glanced towards Reception. Check in, find the room—*he could be working on her self-confidence in less than four minutes.*

'What's the matter? Shouldn't we be going?' She tugged

at his sleeve. 'We don't want to be late. I don't want to miss a single minute of the dancing.'

Torn, Stefano glanced into her sparkling, excited eyes. 'You want to dance?'

'Of course I do. Have you any idea how long it is since I danced?'

'The same length of time since you last had sex?'

'Longer. You're going to have to tear me off the dance floor. I just love the way this dress feels against my skin.' Clearly enjoying her transformation, Liv circled her hips seductively and Stefano inhaled sharply, wondering how he was going to make it through the evening without exploding.

A man seated nearby dropped his glass and it shattered on the marble floor much to the irritation of his large, rather plain wife.

Deciding that he'd better remove Liv from the hotel before she was responsible for more marital disharmony, Stefano drew her arm through his. 'Did they give you a coat of some sort?' He glanced towards the door. 'It's snowing outside. You'll be freezing.'

She turned and picked up a wrap of soft, white fur from the sofa next to them. 'It isn't real fur of course, but it looks amazing, don't you think? It's like being wrapped in a cloud.'

Pleased by the change in her, Stefano smiled. 'What's happened to the woman who loved her elephant pyjamas?'

Liv's eyes sparkled as brightly as the diamonds she was wearing. 'You've corrupted me. I've discovered that being rich and pampered is a life I could enjoy. Does that worry you? Because it probably should. I think I might be about to transform into a greedy, grabbing gold-digger.'

'You have a great deal to learn before you reach the status of gold-digger.' He glanced at his watch. 'We need to leave. The ball started five minutes ago.'

'We're late?'

'Just late enough to make a grand entrance.'

Liv stood at the top of the sweeping staircase that led down to the ballroom. 'Oh my goodness, it's so pretty. I feel really Christmassy all of a sudden.'

Beneath her the room sparkled with festive lights and every table was sprinkled with tiny silver stars and decorated with generous bunches of holly and mistletoe. In the centre of the room a Christmas tree rose up towards the ceiling and a huge star rotated slowly, sending shards of light across the dance floor.

A jazz band was playing Christmas songs to welcome the guests and Liv smiled, so caught up in the excitement of the atmosphere and the sheer indulgence of the moment that it took her a moment to realise that the hum of conversation had dipped and that everyone was staring at her.

'Oh…' Her courage faltered slightly and then she felt Stefano's hand cover hers.

'You're stunning. That's why they're staring.' His tone was amused as he smiled down at her and his smile was so intimate and sexy that she couldn't look away.

'They're probably wondering how long it's going to take me to fall out of this dress,' she muttered. 'I don't want to create a spectacle.'

With a slow, deliberate movement, he pulled her against him and brought his mouth down on hers, kissing her in full view of the entire hospital staff. His kiss was as skilled as it had been that first time and Liv melted like wax under a flame, oblivious to the stir they were causing. It was only when Stefano reluctantly lifted his head that she realised that a dreamy silence had descended on the ballroom. And everyone was still staring.

'I was trying to stay *out* of the limelight,' she said in a strangled voice. 'What do you think you're doing?'

'Staking my claim,' Stefano said calmly, leading her down the stairs. He stopped a waiter, helped himself to two glasses of champagne and handed her one. 'Every man in the room was looking at you. I just wanted to make it clear that you're mine.' His possessive declaration made her stomach flip.

'I'm not yours!'

'Not yet…' The devil danced in his eyes as he lifted his glass in a silent toast. 'But you will be, *tesoro*.'

His words robbed her of thought and breath and Liv forgot about the people watching them. Standing in the full glare of his appreciative masculine gaze, she felt truly beautiful. *And desperately nervous.* He really did seem to be suggesting that— He was implying—

'I've been living under your roof for two weeks and you…' she licked her lips '…you haven't—'

'No, I haven't.' His eyes held hers and a faint smile touched his mouth. 'Max was understandably unsettled by all the changes and I didn't want to make things worse by introducing yet another new factor into his life. I'm assuming from Anna's comments about your sex life that he isn't used to seeing you with a man.'

'So is this what tonight is all about? Are you delivering Anna's Christmas present?'

'This has nothing to do with Anna.' Stefano lifted a lean brown hand and gently brushed his fingers over her cheek. 'This is about us. I'm doing what I've wanted to do since the first moment I laid eyes on you. The past fortnight has been a real test of willpower, believe me.'

Liv had to force herself to breathe. *Stefano Lucarell* *wanted her.* This staggeringly handsome, rich, sophisticate man wanted *her.* And this time she didn't doubt his sincerity because it shimmered in his eyes in a blaze of raw sexuality.

She felt light-headed, dizzy and ecstatic, as if she'd just swallowed the entire glass of champagne in one gulp. Having lived like a nun for four long years, believing that no man would ever find her attractive again, it was a heady experience to suddenly have an incredibly sexy man looking at her in the way Stefano was looking at her. The fact that he wanted her filled her with elation and trepidation.

He didn't love her, she knew that.

She wasn't going to fool herself that for him it was anything more than sexual attraction.

But what was it for her?

She didn't know. She certainly hadn't contemplated another relationship.

And while he was looking at her the way he was looking at her, she couldn't think rationally.

Maybe it didn't matter, she thought helplessly.

Even if she only had this one night, maybe that was just what she needed. Proof that she was an attractive woman. *A boost to her confidence.*

He was still holding her, his strong hand in the centre of her back, his thumb stroking her bare flesh as the chemistry devoured them both. His head was bent towards hers, and she found herself mesmerised by the sheer masculinity of his features. His face was lean and handsome and his jaw was already showing the beginnings of dark shadow, but what really held her attention was the heat in his eyes.

The atmosphere between them was so charged that Liv couldn't think straight. Trying to catch her breath, she placed her hand in the centre of his chest and felt the steady thud of his heart under her fingers. For a moment she was totally lost in him, transfixed by the look in his eyes, seduced by the feel of hard male muscle and warm skin.

Neither of them said a word and yet with look and touch they shared something impossibly intimate and she knew that had they not been in public, it would have been now. Right now. *Right here*.

Stefano said something in Italian and released her with obvious reluctance, and she sensed the sudden dramatic increase in his tension levels.

Breathless, excited and dizzy with longing, Liv was wondering why he'd let her go when she realised that everyone was sitting down to dinner.

As he steered her towards their table, she was hyper-aware of him, her heart rate doubling with every glance he sent her, her skin tingling with anticipation as his arm brushed against hers.

Part of her wanted to be outrageous and suggest in his ear that they just go home, but another part of her was enjoying the glamour, the glitz and the sparkle of the Christmas ball. *And the intoxicating, dizzying knowledge that Stefano Lucarelli wanted her.*

She felt irresistible, and she wanted the feeling to last for ever.

It was hard to give any attention to the man seated on her other side because for her no one existed except for Stefano and just the thought of what was to come made her stomach perform acrobatics.

The waiters removed her first course untouched and then served her main course.

'I thought working mothers need carbohydrates.' Lifting his glass to his lips, Stefano glanced at her untouched plate. 'What has happened to your appetite? You're not hungry, *tesoro*?'

'No.' Her stomach performed another flip. 'Not really.'

He rose to his feet and held out his hand. 'Then let's dance.'

Liv wasn't sure that her legs would hold her but she let him lead her onto the dance floor.

He curved her against him in a decisive, possessive gesture that made her heart skip. Brought into close contact with his lean, hard body, she felt an unfamiliar flash of heat explode inside her. Her hands slid upwards to his powerful shoulders and then locked around his neck.

The music had tempted quite a few couples onto the dance floor, but Liv was oblivious to everyone except Stefano and she had a feeling that that was exactly the way he wanted it.

The anticipation of what was to come was almost suffocating. Warmth spread through her pelvis, turning her limbs to liquid and Liv gave a little shiver and slid her hands through the hair at the back of his neck.

The tension levels between them had reached the point of explosion and when a shower of tiny silver stars drifted onto the dance floor drawing gasps of delight from all around them, Stefano finally eased her away from him and stared down at her.

'Time to go home, I think,' he breathed softly and guided her back to the table. They collected her bag and her wrap and left the ballroom to find the limousine waiting.

Liv slid into the warmth of the luxurious interior, but it was impossible to relax. Instead of savouring every second of the experience, she found herself desperate to arrive at his apartment and she suspected he was experiencing a similar degree of urgency because he suddenly lifted a hand, undid his tie and loosened his top button.

His eyes met hers for a brief, electrifying moment and she felt that look right through her body.

Why was she feeling this way?

Was it just because she hadn't had sex for such a very long time?

Or was it something more?

She didn't know. All she knew was that being with him felt right. Slightly scary, but right.

Outside, the streets of London were eerily empty, the snowfall muffling sounds and giving the city an ethereal quality that seemed to add to the tension of the moment. Shop windows shone and sparkled with festive decorations as the car purred silently through the wintry atmosphere and emerged in Knightsbridge.

Her high heels echoed on the marble floor of his apartment building, the sound reminding her of a dramatic drum roll announcing the grand finale of the evening. It was only as they walked into the lift and Stefano pressed the button for the top floor that reality hit her.

Suddenly consumed by a violent attack of nerves, Liv tried to extract her hand from Stefano's, but his fingers held her firmly.

'You are glamorous and beautiful and stop thinking otherwise.'

Wondering how he could read her so easily, she shot him an embarrassed glance. 'Am I that transparent?'

'Yes,' he murmured, his eyes surprisingly gentle. 'Unlike most women, you are refreshingly easy to understand.'

'It's the dress that's glamorous and beautiful,' she said in a strangled voice. 'Underneath, I'm still me.'

'I really hope so. I'm relying on that fact.' Turning her to face him, Stefano slid his hands over the curve of her bottom and drew her against him. And then he brought his mouth down on hers.

He'd kissed her before, but this time felt different. The desire had been building between them all evening and this time there was no gentle promise or slow, sensual hint of more to come. This time his kiss was a declaration of intent, a skilled deliberate assault on her senses designed to trigger a similarly explosive response from her. There was a whisper of silk as he slid the silver dress up her thigh with a purposeful movement of his hand and then his mouth moved to her neck and lower still.

The lift doors opened and Liv gave a gasp of surprise as he scooped her easily into his arms and carried her into his apartment.

'Stefano, you can't—' Her faint protest was smothered by the possessive demands of his mouth and her wrap slid to the floor, closely followed by the silver bag.

Without lifting his head from hers, he carried her through to his bedroom and then lowered her gently to the floor.

Beyond the huge glass windows stretched the winter wonderland that was Hyde Park, but Liv was so dazed from his kiss and from the look in his glittering dark eyes that she couldn't focus on anything except him. For her, Christmas was in this apartment, with this man.

Cupping her face in his hands, Stefano brought his mouth down on hers again and this time she just melted against him, so excited that she could hardly breathe. He kissed her slowly and thoroughly and with such skill and expertise that her body threatened to explode. Lost in his kiss, she barely felt the sensual slide of his strong hands over her body and when her dress pooled on the floor she gave a murmur of shock and pulled away slightly.

'Stefano—'

'You have the most amazing body,' he said hoarsely and the raw appreciation in his eyes doused the sudden flicker of insecurity that had threatened to disturb the moment.

He tipped her back onto the bed and came down on top of her, his expert hands tracing every contour of her shivering, excited body. His mouth lingered on the sliver of lace that framed the tantalising dip between her breasts and then suddenly she was naked from the waist up, totally exposed to his disturbing masculine gaze.

Blindly wondering how he managed to undress her without her even noticing, Liv was just about to protest when he drew his tongue over one pink-tipped nipple and she felt a spasm of sexual heat connecting with the most intimate part of her. With a moan of disbelief, she arched against his clever mouth and with the skilled flick of his tongue and fingers he drove all traces of shyness from her brain.

Liv was no longer thinking about the fact that she was virtually naked. Neither did she care that the moon was providing sufficient light for him to enjoy a leisurely visual survey of her body.

Her body ached and throbbed and she writhed her hips against the silk sheets, needing him to touch her but far too shy to ask. The air vibrated with sexual tension but Stefano took his time, driving her to screaming pitch with the deliberate touch of his mouth and his fingers. When he slowly drew away from her and stood up, she almost sobbed out a protest and then realised that he was removing his own clothes. His eyes didn't once leave hers as he swiftly dispensed with his shirt and dropped those lean, clever fingers to the button of his trousers.

His chest was broad and muscular, the bronzed skin darkened with crisp curls of male hair that drew the eye inexorably downwards over his board-flat abdomen to the bold thrust of his erection.

He discarded his clothes in a careless heap and his firm mouth curved into a sexy smile full of masculine promise.

The mattress dipped as he came down beside her and Liv felt her stomach knot in wicked anticipation as he slid a hard, muscular thigh over her legs, trapping her.

'Do you know how long I have waited for this?' With an appreciative murmur, he slid a leisurely hand down her body and Liv shivered with helpless longing.

She would have expected to feel self-conscious, but he was looking at her with such a blaze of sexual hunger that it was impossible to feel anything other than beautiful and seductive.

When his clever mouth closed over one pink nipple she gasped, and as his warm, strong hand slid confidently over her thigh she shifted her hips to try and relieve the nagging ache that was building inside her.

She didn't feel like herself. *Everything* about her world suddenly seemed different. She was hot, burning and just dizzy with longing as he introduced her to an eroticism that she'd never before known.

Her fingers slid over the hard muscle of his shoulders and he lifted his head and looked at her, his glittering eyes half-shielded by thick, black lashes.

'You are spectacular.' He shifted slightly and brought his mouth down on hers and every single part of her shivered and quivered with agonising sexual tension. Their eyes held as his tongue danced with hers and Liv squirmed underneath him, her thigh sliding against the rough hardness of his.

His hand slid between her legs and she cried out as she felt the expert stroke of his fingers touching her moist femininity. The pleasure was so wickedly intense that the world around her suddenly ceased to exist and there was nothing but him.

'Stefano…' She gasped his name against his mouth in a desperate plea and he shifted her underneath him in a swift, decisive move.

'I need you now,' he groaned thickly, 'I can't wait.'

Liv felt the hard probe of his erection against her and dug her nails into his shoulder. As she arched her hips towards him, he slid his hand into her hair and for a moment he stared down into her eyes, his gaze fierce and hot. Then he shifted his weight and sank into her with a purposeful thrust that drew a harsh groan from the back of his throat and a startled gasp from her.

He was powerfully male and for a moment the feel of him inside her was so overwhelming that she couldn't move or breathe. His eyes were dark and demanding, the atmosphere was steamy and hot and each thrust of his body drove her deeper and deeper into an ecstasy that she'd never known before.

The excitement bordered on terrifying and as he drove her higher and higher she clung to the hard muscle of his shoulders. Consumed by unbearable pleasure, her world exploded in a shower of exquisite sensation and her body tightened around his as she fell, spiralling down and down in a dizzying, endless tumble of ecstasy.

Stefano groaned in agonising pleasure and reached his own peak, his passion so intense and demanding that it prolonged her own pulsing excitement. Liv wrapped her arms around him, holding him as tightly as he was holding her, shocked and dazed by sensation and wishing that they could stay like this for ever.

She woke to bright sunshine and the knowledge that she was naked in Stefano's arms.

Memories of the night before filled her head but her initial rush of elation was swiftly swamped by her old feelings of insecurity. Conscious that moonlight created a very different atmosphere from the harsh honesty of daylight, Liv felt a sudden desperate urge to put some clothes on and wondered how she was going to extract herself without waking him up.

The fabulous silver dress still lay in a pool on the floor, a reminder that the magical night was well and truly over.

Willing him not to open his eyes, she turned her head to look at him. He was intensely masculine and for a moment her gaze lingered on the hard lines of his face and his firm, sensual mouth. His lashes were thick and dark and his jaw was blue with stubble. Even in sleep he was breathtakingly, impossibly handsome and her insides squirmed as she remembered the intimacies they'd shared the night before.

How could she have ever thought that one night with this man would be enough?

The trouble with discovering the existence of really, really good sex, she thought to herself, *was that one didn't want to give it up.*

No wonder women were disgruntled when he ended a relationship. They knew that they'd just lost perfection.

And now she had to find a way of leaving the bed without disturbing him.

Gently and slowly she tried to ease away from him but he tightened his grip and pulled her back against him. 'Where do you think you're going?'

Agonisingly aware of the brush of his thigh against hers, she stilled. 'I was going to get dressed.'

'Don't bother,' he murmured softly, rolling her underneath him and combing her hair away from her face with a gentle hand. 'We don't have to collect Max until four o'clock. That gives us all day.'

Her heart thudding, she stared up at him. 'I'm naked.'

'I know, *tesoro*. And you are beautiful. *Molto bella*.' With a sexy smile, he shifted his body subtly and she gasped as she felt the hard thrust of his arousal.

'Stefano—'

He lowered his head and kissed her mouth, cutting her off before she could say what she wanted to say. 'You have a glorious, fabulous body and to let you wear clothes would be criminally irresponsible.'

'I was going to have a shower,' she murmured, distracted by the touch of his mouth on her neck. How did he know exactly where to touch her?

'Good idea. We'll take one together.' Delivering a last, lingering kiss on her mouth, Stefano sprang out of bed, gloriously naked and as confident and unselfconscious as ever.

Maybe if she looked as good as him, she'd be confident too, Liv thought and then gave a gasp of shock as he swung her into his arms.

Ignoring her muttered confession that she'd never showered with anyone before, he carried her into his enormous bathroom and lowered her gently to the floor. Then he hit a button on the wall and jets of deliciously warm water cascaded over both of them.

'The great thing about showering *with* someone,' he said, his Italian accent suddenly very pronounced, 'is that they do all the work.' Reaching for the soap, he gave a her a wicked smile and slid his hands slowly and deliberately over her body. 'Tell me—what is it that you don't like about your body?'

'I don't know, I can't think when you're doing that to me!' She tilted her head back and then gasped as the water hit her full in the face. 'I'm drowning…'

Laughing, he nudged her gently back against the wall of the shower, away from the direct flow of the jets of water. 'Better?'

She opened her mouth to answer but then his hand slid

between her thighs and the only sound she was capable of making was a low moan of pleasure and desperation. The water flowed over her but she was only aware of the expert slide of his fingers against her flesh. His touch was wickedly skilled and when he dropped to his knees in front of her, she gave a whimper of disbelief.

She had to stop him. She knew she had to stop him but then he parted her gently and the only sound that emerged was a low moan of pleasure.

The heated, moist sensation of his mouth drove the breath from her body and every rational thought from her head as he licked her with slow strokes of his tongue and then teasing flickers that drove her wild with desire.

Her pelvis ached and throbbed and she moved restlessly, overtaken by the heat that he was creating. The tremors started to engulf her and then he slid his fingers deep and she exploded into an orgasm so intense that for a moment the world went black and she forgot where she was and who she was with. She lost control totally and it felt like endless minutes before she was finally able to open her eyes and look at him.

Stefano rose to his feet, paused long enough to protect her and then he put his hands under her hips and lifted her, his eyes impossibly dark and slumberous as he held her gaze. 'I think you are fabulous and beautiful, Liv—' His voice was husky. 'Are you getting the message yet?' His arms and shoulders were thickened with muscle and he held her easily, his erection hot and heavy against her as he positioned her to his satisfaction. His strong fingers bit hard into her thighs and she cried out in ecstasy as he surged into her body with a single, decisive thrust. She felt the warmth and fullness of him deep, deep inside her and he paused for a moment as sexual chemistry threatened to devour them both. Stefano groaned something in Italian and withdrew slightly, only to thrust again, this time deeper than the last time. Holding her securely, he began a sensual, erotic rhythm that felt so agonisingly, impossibly good that Liv felt the immediate response of her body. She wanted to move her hips but he was the one in control, his body pressed hard against hers, his shoulders and arms taking her weight as he drove into her again and again. Ripples of exquisite excitement turned to an explosion of ecstasy and she felt him shudder against her as her own body was suddenly showered with sensation.

She clung to him, ignoring the drenching flow of the shower and the relentless patter of her heartbeat. It was only when he finally lowered her gently to the floor and smiled at her that she realised just how much trouble she was in.

Nothing was ever going to be the same again. How could it be after a night with this man? Before the previous night she'd managed to convince herself that she was happy being single, that her life with her little boy was enough. All her fulfilment and satisfaction had come from her role as a mother and she hadn't dared explore the world beyond. She'd been too afraid. Jack's cruel rejection had acted like chains, preventing her from exploring her needs as a woman.

But one night with Stefano had set her free from those restraints.

With soft words and skilled touch, he'd made her feel like a beautiful, confident woman and she knew that she'd never again be able to shut that part of herself down. She wanted to share her life with a man, but not just any man.

Stefano.

Which meant that she was heading for disaster, because this was a man who had confessed himself unable to find that one special woman.

CHAPTER NINE

'I NEED you to look straight ahead,' Liv said gently, her hands holding the child's as she coaxed the little boy to do as she wanted. 'Mr Lucarelli is going to look in your eyes. Good boy.'

'That light thing feels funny.'

'Don't think about the light thing. Think about me, instead. Tell me what you're hoping to have for Christmas.' She kept the conversation going, hoping that she looked and sounded normal. She certainly didn't feel normal. *Everything* about her had changed. Her view of life, her view of herself, her view of her body...

'A skateboard.'

'Wow!' Liv let go of one of his hands so that she could hand Stefano the equipment he needed. She was careful not to look at him. If she looked at him then she thought of sex and if she started thinking about sex, then she wouldn't be able to concentrate. She was desperate to ask him what was going to happen now, but at the same time she didn't dare because she was so afraid of the answer. For him it had been a fling, she was sure of that. And there hadn't even been an opportunity to continue the relationship because Max was now back in the apartment. 'A skateboard? That is fantastic. Have you ever been on one before?'

'Once. At my cousin's house. I fell off and hurt my arm.'

'Better make sure you ask Father Christmas for some protective pads then, and a good helmet. Tilt your head for us slightly, good boy.' Liv moved slightly so that Stefano could get a better view. Was he finding it as difficult as she was? No, apparently not. In public he was his usual cool, composed self, but in private…

She gave a tiny smile, thinking of the long conversations they'd shared after Max had fallen asleep, curled up together on his deep, comfortable sofa. Conversations designed to take their minds off the powerful attraction that drew them together. Liv didn't feel comfortable making love while Max was in the apartment and she suspected that Stefano felt the same way because he hadn't pushed the point. And he still wanted her, she knew he did. Maybe they could find an opportunity. Maybe she could talk to Anna—

'Drops, Liv.' Stefano's tone was impatient and she gave a start and handed him the drops, allowing herself a slight smile. Even their special relationship didn't allow her any concessions when it came to efficiency.

'Do you want him to have an eye patch?' She forced her mind back to the job and smiled at the little boy. 'I hope Father Christmas brings you everything you want.'

'That's fine. I'm done. No eye patch, but I want him to have chloramphenicol.' Stefano stepped away from the little boy and ripped off his gloves. 'Well done, Nick. You were very brave. There's a little scratch in your eye but we'll give you some ointment to help.'

His mother stood up. 'He needs a prescription?'

Stefano talked to her about the care Nick was going to need and then strolled out of the cubicle.

Counting the hours until they could go home, Liv sorted

out the eye ointment, gave them an advice sheet to take home and then went back to tidy the cubicle.

Moments later, Anna slid into the room. 'All right, I've had enough of this. I want to know everything.'

'Everything about what?'

'Liv, I've waited *four days* for you to tell me what happened on the night of the ball, but you've been avoiding me. I gave up my ticket so that you could go. The least you can do is tell me whether my sacrifice was worth it. Judging from the smile on your face, I'm guessing that it was.'

'I had a nice time, yes. I've already told you that. The food was great…' *even though she hadn't eaten any* '…and the band was fantastic.'

'I'm not remotely interested in the band or the food. *I want to know about Stefano.*'

Just the sound of his name sent a tiny thrill through her body. 'I had a lovely time.'

'Lovely time?' Anna gritted her teeth. 'You spent the night with the sexiest man on the planet and all you can say is that you had a lovely time? How much of a lovely time?'

'It was nice.'

'Nice? What sort of feedback is that? I want details! Did you—you know…?' Anna waggled her eyebrows suggestively. 'Please tell me you did. I'm guessing that you did, because you're suddenly smiling all the time.'

'Anna!' Liv blushed. 'I am *not* answering that!'

'So obviously you did.' Anna rested her bottom on the table, a satisfied smile on her face. 'Well? Were you a buttoned-up prude or a brazen hussy?'

'Oh, definitely a brazen hussy,' Liv said lightly, remembering the raw explosive passion they'd shared.

Anna sighed. 'Thank goodness for that. Tell me about it.'

'He's wonderful,' Liv said simply. 'I know he can be controlling sometimes, but to be honest I quite like that because I'm totally exhausted with having to make every decision by myself. I've discovered that sometimes it's just wonderful to let someone take over. And he *really* cares about Max. He has nephews Max's age and he really understands how they—'

'Yes, yes, I know he's good with kids, I've seen him in Resus,' Anna said impatiently. '*But what about the sex?* Was he amazing?'

Amazing? No, he'd been more than just amazing. Liv's legs trembled. 'It would be totally wrong of me to talk about that.'

'That good, hmm?' Anna grinned. 'And did he have stamina?'

Liv's face turned scarlet. 'Anna, for goodness' sake…'

'All right, now I'm starting to hate you.' Anna's laughter faded and she studied her friend. 'And there was me, worrying that when it came to the crucial moment, you'd refuse to take your clothes off.'

'I didn't even think about it,' Liv said honestly. 'He made me feel—beautiful.'

'That's because you are beautiful. Believe me, the guy isn't doing you a favour. He's struck gold and he knows it. And I have to say, I'm loving the new you.'

'I'm loving the new me, too.' Liv glanced sideways to check that no one was listening and gave a secretive smile. 'I feel alive. I adored the life I had with Max, but it was hard and I can't pretend otherwise. I used to lie awake at night worrying about the boiler going and not being able to afford the repair, and now I'm awake at night because I'm thinking about—' She broke off and Anna groaned.

'All right, enough or I'll punch you. So what happens now? You carry on having hot sex over Christmas?'

Liv turned and dropped the remains of the dressing pack into the bin. 'No. Obviously we have Max to think of.'

Anna gaped at her. 'So you haven't done it since...' She waved a hand. 'You're kidding.'

'No.' Liv rubbed her fingers over her forehead. 'It's not just about the two of us, Anna. Max has just had a huge amount of change in his life. I'm worried it will upset him.'

'He loves Stefano. He talks about him all the time.'

'I know he loves him, but that still doesn't mean I want him to see Stefano and I in bed together. It just doesn't feel right.'

'So now I know why Stefano's fuse is even shorter than usual,' Anna said dryly. 'What does he say about the situation?'

'We haven't talked about the future, if that's what you mean.' Liv walked across to the sink and washed her hands. 'I don't know what's going to happen. But the flat won't be habitable for a couple of months at least because there was some structural damage.'

'Well the two of you aren't going to be able to keep your hands off each other for that long. You're crazy about him, aren't you?'

Liv didn't even bother denying it. 'I don't think I'm one of those women who can just have a night of hot sex and move on. For me it's—' She swallowed. 'It's emotional.'

'So basically you love him.'

Liv looked away, shocked by how those words sounded and felt. 'Don't be ridiculous,' she said hoarsely. 'I've only known him for a few weeks.'

'Time is irrelevant as we both know. Does he feel the same way?'

Liv stared at the poster on the wall without seeing it. 'I think he cares about me.'

The sound of an ambulance siren disturbed their conversation and Liv glanced behind her. 'Are we expecting someone?'

'Child with a temperature. Greg is going to see him to begin with but I've asked Stefano to check on things when he's free. He's been keeping a close eye on Greg, as you know. In the meantime you'd better get in there and do your stuff. A few weeks under the boss's eye has improved Greg's performance, but he's still far too reluctant to ask for help.'

'I'll go. I need distraction.' Liv washed her hands and glanced at her friend with a soft smile. 'All I seem to think about now is sex and it's all your fault.'

'I know. I'm so pleased with myself. I'm going to give up my job and run a dating agency.'

Laughing, Liv walked out of the room and hurried towards Resus. She was still smiling when she opened the swing doors but the smile faded the instant she saw the little boy seated on his mother's lap. He was ominously quiet and was leaning with his chin slightly forward, as if he was sniffing something.

Liv's instincts screamed a warning and she turned to Greg, ready to voice her concerns.

'Dr Hampton, I think we should—'

'Great, now you're here, I can examine him.' Although Greg's tone was civil enough, she could see the flash of irritation in his eyes. 'I've taken a history but I want to lay him down on the trolley so that I can take a proper look.'

'No, don't move him!' Realising from the sudden tightening of his mouth that she'd overstepped the mark, Liv tried again. 'He's probably best on his mother's lap for now,' she said tactfully, knowing that the child had chosen the position that was most comfortable for him. 'I expect you want me to give him some humidified oxygen.' As she dealt with that, she glanced swiftly at the notes, checking mother's and child's names. 'Hello, Tom. You're obviously feeling very poorly, sweetheart.'

The child made no attempt to respond and Liv adjusted the flow of oxygen and then turned to the mother. 'Has he been like this for long, Kelly?'

'He was fine yesterday. I think he's just fussing.' The mother sounded tired and irritable. 'He just wants a bit of sympathy.' She was little more than a child herself and Liv could see that she had no idea how sick her little boy was. Unfortunately, Greg didn't appear aware of it, either.

'Has your GP seen him?'

'Are you kidding?' The girl rolled her eyes. 'Couldn't get an appointment. To start with I thought Tom was just playing up because he didn't want to go to school, then he felt hot so I thought I'd bring him down and get him checked. He had me up all night and I'm not going through that again tonight. He's really clingy. I just want you to give him something to sort him out.'

'Let's get him on the trolley,' Greg said briskly but Liv gave a brief shake of her head and took him to one side, knowing that they were dealing with a potentially life-threatening situation.

'Greg.' She kept her voice soft so that neither child nor mother could overhear her words. 'This child has serious breathing problems. We shouldn't move him. He's naturally adopted the position that's most comfortable for him, which is upright. I expect you'd like me to call an anaesthetist and an ENT surgeon right now.' She'd phrased it in such a way that he could simply agree without losing face, but his eyes narrowed defensively.

'I'll make that judgement if and when it needs to be made. You're overreacting. There is no stridor and no cough.'

'I'm aware of that, but…' Liv bit her lip and swiftly questioned her own judgement. *Was she overreacting?* 'It's the way he's holding his head. I think he could have epiglottitis. I've seen it once before.'

'I've already taken a history and he's been fully immunised.'

'It could be a vaccine failure.'

'The haemophilus influenza vaccine is ninety-eight per cent effective,' Greg said impatiently and Liv nodded.

'I know that. I know it's unlikely. But I also know what I'm seeing and to be honest the question "why" is irrelevant at the moment. This child is showing signs of progressive airway obstruction and we need to deal with that. Fast.'

Greg leaned towards her, his eyes hard. 'Sorry, but am I the doctor here, or are you?'

'You, but I've worked in the emergency department for five years and—'

'And perhaps you've become addicted to drama. Five years here still doesn't make you a doctor.' He smiled pleasantly. 'I'll examine him. Then I'll decide who to refer him to. And I'll let you know so that you can make the call.'

Her heart pounded because she absolutely *hated* conflict and normally would have done everything possible to avoid it. *But this was different.* She knew that any delay could be serious.

Where was Stefano?

Hadn't Anna said that she'd asked him to check the child?

She glanced towards the little boy, knowing that if anything happened to him because she hadn't acted, she wouldn't be able to live with herself.

Feeling physically sick at the thought of what she was about to do, Liv moved towards the phone, ignoring Greg's fierce warning glare. As she called Switchboard and asked for them to emergency bleep the on-call anaesthetist and the ENT surgeon, her hands were shaking and she wondered how she was ever going to be able to salvage her working relationship with the junior doctor. *He was due to leave in January*, she reminded herself. She just had to get through another few weeks. And even if he never spoke to her again, it didn't matter.

Pushing aside that worry for later, she checked the child's weight from the notes and reached for an ampoule of adrenaline just as Stefano strode into the room.

'Anna asked me to see a patient?' He looked as cool and confident as ever, the blue scrub suit emphasising the width and power of his shoulders and Liv had never been so pleased to see anyone in her life. She felt her limbs weaken, but this time it was not because he was exceptionally good-looking but simply because she needed senior back-up and one glance at Stefano inspired confidence.

Kelly's eyes widened and she transformed from being tired and irritable to alert and interested. Instinctively she lifted a hand and smoothed her hair but Stefano wasn't looking at her. He was looking at the child. And that one look was clearly enough for him, as it had been for Liv.

He focused his gaze on Greg. 'Have you bleeped the on-call anaesthetist and the ENT surgeon?'

The colour drained from Greg's cheeks and he stood a little straighter. 'Yes,' he muttered and Stefano relaxed slightly and nodded his approval.

'Good.' He turned to Liv. 'Let's give him nebulised adrenaline.'

'I have it here.' She handed him the tray and showed him the ampoule. 'I've checked his weight and given him point-five millilitres per kilogram. Are you happy with that?'

'Give it.' Having delegated that task, Stefano crouched down next to the child, his eyes gentle. 'You are having problems with your breathing, but we are going to help you with that.'

Greg cleared his throat. 'Do you want to do a lateral chest X-ray?'

'In this case it's not necessary and potentially hazardous.' Stefano straightened and looked at Liv. 'I want a 16-gauge cannula ready.'

'I already have it.' As always, her mind had been working along the same lines as his. She knew that he was afraid that the child's airway might become completely obstructed and he wanted to ensure that everything was within reach so that he could create an airway with the needle if he had to.

'Cefotaxime?'

'I have that ready, too, but I thought you might like to wait until the anaesthetist has assessed him.'

Stefano gave a faint smile and was about to comment when the anaesthetist walked into the room along with the ENT consultant.

It was another hour before the child was stabilised and transferred out of the emergency department.

'Greg.' Stefano's tone was cool and businesslike. 'You need to talk to the mother about contacts and arrange treatment. You did well. A case of epiglottitis is extremely rare, but still you considered it and managed the case accordingly. You didn't sit the child up, you didn't examine the throat and you called for help early. I'm impressed.'

Greg's gaze flickered to Liv and she looked at him, waiting for him to tell the truth. But the doctor simply smiled.

'Thanks. Good teamwork, Liv. I'll go and talk to the mother about antibiotic cover.'

He left the room and Liv turned away, struggling with an unpleasant ethical dilemma. If she hadn't acted, Greg's actions could have put the patient in danger. She had to say something but it felt like a very uncomfortable thing to do.

'So…' Stefano's accented drawl came from directly behind her. 'Having just established that Greg Hampton is a coward who is afraid to take responsibility for his own actions, I'm relying on you to have the courage to tell me the truth about what just happened in here.'

Liv turned slowly. 'You knew?'

'Did you really think that I wouldn't sense that something was going on? You were panicking when I walked into the room,' he said softly, his dark eyes fixed on her face, 'and I've never seen you panic before. And Greg kept looking at you as if he was afraid you might say something you shouldn't. So, I'll ask you the question once again. What happened here?'

Liv took a deep breath. 'Dr Hampton and I had a slight difference of opinion over the correct management of the patient.'

'Who rang the anaesthetist?' Stefano studied her face for a moment and then his mouth tightened. 'You, obviously.'

Feeling slightly shaky, Liv took a deep breath. 'I went over his head. I shouldn't have done it, I know, but—'

'You were absolutely right to do it.' Stefano's tone was cool and unemotional. 'In this department we put patient welfare before staff egos. That child could have died.'

'You think I did the right thing?'

'You know you did.'

'I suppose I do, but that doesn't stop me feeling very bad about it,' she confessed. 'I've never had an incident like that in five years of working here. Normally doctors are happy to work as a team and exchange ideas, but Dr Hampton never—'

'He never listens. And he thinks he's always right. I'll deal with it. It's no longer your problem.' He looked at her thoughtfully and then frowned slightly. 'You're shaking. Is that because of the medical emergency?'

'No.' Exasperated with herself, she gave a shrug. 'It's because I hate confrontation. Pathetic, isn't it?'

'It isn't pathetic. It's what makes you who you are.' His sexy mouth curved slightly. 'You're gentle and caring and I really love that. Forget Dr Hampton. I will deal with him.'

Now that the crisis was over she was suddenly very aware of him and it was a struggle to keep her eyes averted from the hint of bronzed male skin visible at the neck of the scrub suit.

Having not thought about sex for years, suddenly she was thinking about nothing else.

Stefano's gaze lingered on her flushed cheeks and then his hand closed around her wrist and he hauled her against him.

'If I don't kiss you, I'm going to explode,' he breathed and brought his mouth down on hers in a hard, possessive kiss that sent hungry tremors through her body.

'Stefano...' She wrapped her arms round his neck and kissed him back, oblivious to everything except the shocking expertise of his kiss. It was hot, explosive and out of control and it was only the sound of voices outside the door that made them both break apart.

'*Accidenti.*' Stefano released her suddenly and raked his hands through his hair. 'I have never before kissed a woman at work. That's how desperate I am,' he muttered and she found herself unable to breathe.

'You're desperate?'

'Do you doubt it? Soon I will be ready to give Max the keys to my Ferrari in exchange for an hour alone with you. It's Christmas in three days' time and neither of us is working.' His eyes dropped to her mouth. 'I'm taking you to Italy. We'll spend the holiday at the chalet. I want to take you to meet my family.'

He wanted her to meet his family?

Joy, hope and excitement mingled together in a dizzying cocktail that made her head spin.

Would he take her to meet his family if their relationship meant nothing more to him than sex? Suddenly her mind was full of questions, but she had no opportunity to ask any of them because Stefano cast an impatient glance at his watch.

'I have a meeting with the chief executive in ten minutes and I need to talk to Greg.' He looked back at her. 'Go shopping. Use the card I gave you and buy plenty of warm clothes. Max is going to have snow for Christmas.'

CHAPTER TEN

'YOU'RE going to Italy to stay with his family?' Anna handed a set of notes to a nurse who was passing. 'Well that sounds like happily ever after if ever I heard it.'

'Not really.' Liv was trying to keep a lid on her excitement. 'I mean, he can hardly leave us alone in his flashy apartment, ʾan he? We'd set off all the alarms.'

'And you think that's the reason he's taking you home to ꞏt his dad and sister at Christmas? I don't think so. Don't ꞏremember that interview with the actress? She said that ꞏever taken a woman to meet his family.'

'ꞏ it, Anna.' Liv covered her ears with her hands. 'Stop ꞏne hope.'

'ꞏ wrong with hope? Hope is what stops us all from ꞏthe tracks. Trust me.' Anna lowered her voice. 'ꞏgood-looking guy takes you to meet his family, ꞏd dry. I smell diamonds for Christmas. Except ꞏn you diamonds. More diamonds, then. Have ꞏhow much I hate you?'

'ꞏg. 'Enough!' She walked away from her ꞏnation was already working overtime, as ꞏissued the invitation.

ꞏn more of a command than an invitation, she thought wryly, which was typical of Stefano. But command or invitation, it held meaning.

It wasn't even as if he was taking her to some anonymous hotel somewhere. He was taking her to meet his family and obviously that wasn't something he did with every woman he met.

They hadn't actually spoken about their feelings, that was true, but wasn't it true that actions spoke louder than words? Surely the fact that he was taking her home to meet his family must mean something?

Excitement bubbled up inside her and she tried desperately to squash it down.

'How does it stay in the sky? Where are all the other passengers?' Max bounced in his seat, so excited that he was finding it impossible to sit still. 'Are we in Italy yet?'

Stefano watched him with amusement. 'There are no other passengers because this plane is owned by my family, we're not in Italy yet and we stay in the sky because—' He broke off and exhaled slowly. 'I don't know what level of explanation is suitable for a seven-year-old.'

'Just tell me,' Max said earnestly. 'If it's too complicated, I'll say so.'

Listening to Stefano talk about thrust and lift, Liv smiled to herself. It was utter bliss to allow someone else the privilege of delivering simple answers to complicated questions.

Max was transfixed. 'And what happens if—?'

'That's enough, Max.' Liv intervened finally. 'You've been firing questions at Stefano since we took off from the airport. Aren't you tired? Wouldn't you like a nap?'

'Babies nap. I'm seven, Mum.' Max gave her a pitying look and then slipped his hand into Stefano's. 'What are we going to do when we land? Are we going to the mountains straight away? Will there be enough snow to build a snowman? Can I go sledging?'

'You can do all those things.' Stefano glanced at his watch. 'Providing that we are not delayed.' He stretched his legs out in front of him and Liv quickly looked away, wishing that every movement he made didn't remind her of the night of the ball.

She really needed to get herself under control before she met his family, otherwise she was going to embarrass both of them.

As Stefano drove the last few kilometres towards the chalet, Max was bouncing in his seat.

'I didn't know this much snow existed anywhere. In London we just have a tiny bit, never enough for a snowman. It's all over the roads and the roofs and it's higher than me.' His tone was awed as he gazed around him. 'Now I see why you had to use a four-wheel drive.'

'The Ferrari is not designed for winter in the mountains.' Stefano took another hairpin bend and slowed down. 'We're here.'

In her mind, Liv had imagined a tiny log cabin but the home in front of her was something entirely different. A traditional wooden chalet with a sloping roof buried under a least a foot of snow, it was sheltered to one side by tall fir trees and surrounded by a beautifully carved wooden balcony. Beneath them in the valley she could see the sparkling lights of the village and a church.

'It's stunning.'

'The village is pretty crowded at this time of year, so being up here away from the hordes is a good thing. But we'll go down tomorrow and I'll show you around.' He parked the car and switched off the engine. 'Max will like it. Horse-drawn sleighs, ice skating—pretty much a child's heaven.'

And an adult's heaven too, Liv thought wistfully as she jumped down from the car. It was easily the most beautiful, peaceful place she'd ever seen. There was no sound apart from the soft crunch as their feet broke through the fragile crust of snow and the occasional muffled thud as lumps of snow fell from the heavily laden trees onto the ground below.

She breathed in, loving the smell of woodsmoke and pine trees. The cold air stung her cheeks and Liv gave a little shiver as she reached out her arms to lift Max down from the car.

'Mum, have you seen the snow?' Max was almost incoherent with excitement and Liv smiled.

'I've seen it. In fact I'm standing in it and my feet are cold. Hurry up.'

Stefano swung two of the cases out of the boot. 'Most of these snowdrifts are probably deeper than you are tall so don't wander off.'

For a man who didn't have children he was remarkably in tune with the way children thought. And then she remembered that he worked in the emergency department and was constantly exposed to the consequences of a child's need to explore and push the boundaries.

'Can we build a snowman now?' Max bent down and started to scoop snow into his palms. 'This is awesome.' He straightened and Liv caught the mischievous look in his eye too late to avoid the inevitable snowball.

She gasped and closed her eyes as a freezing shower of snow smacked into her hair and trickled down her neck. 'Oh my goodness, that's *freezing*! Max you are in serious trouble now!' Her eyes glinted and she stooped and gathered her own ball of snow while Max squealed in delighted terror.

Giggling like a child, Liv carefully lobbed the snowball into the middle of his back, where she knew it would cause the least damage in terms of wet and cold. Then she caught Stefano's gaze and smiled. 'Sorry. I'm as bad as he is, I know. It's just that neither of us have seen snow like this before. It's like waking up in the middle of a fairy-tale.'

But the best part of the fairy-tale was being here with him.

The door of the chalet suddenly opened sending shafts of bright light across the snow. There was a chorus of welcome and then suddenly there were people everywhere and they were engulfed by hugging, kissing, laughter and lots of unintelligible Italian.

Overwhelmed, Max dropped the snow he'd been holding and shrank against Liv. She slid an arm round him, feeling equally daunted by the noisy exuberance of Stefano's *extremely* large family. Two big dogs bounded towards them and Stefano spoke a sharp command in Italian. Both of them skidded to a halt, sending soft snow showering everywhere. Then they whimpered and sat, watching him expectantly.

'Are they friendly?' Still holding onto Liv, Max gazed at the dogs in fascination and Stefano dropped to his haunches next to him.

'*Sì*, they are friendly. Put your hand out and let them smell you.'

Max stuck his hand out and both dogs sidled towards him and licked him frantically, their tails sending more snow flying in all directions. 'Ew!' Giggling and cringing at the same time, Max jerked his hand away. 'That's so wet. It's gross.' But he was enchanted by the dogs, and the animals were enough to break the ice.

'This is all a bit much for you, I'm so sorry.' A dark-haired woman with a warm smile pulled Liv towards her and kissed ner on both cheeks. 'It's just that we don't see enough of Stefano. You're *very* welcome. I'm his sister, Isabella.' She miled at Max. 'The dogs are Leo and Angelo. Everyone else an be introduced at some other point. It's freezing out here. Let's go inside.'

Dinner was a noisy, lengthy affair with simultaneous conversations and much friendly argument and disagreement.

Stefano's father, Bernardo, sat at the head of the table watching over the proceedings like a benign monarch. Occasionally Liv caught his warm, approving gaze and she wondered exactly what Stefano had said about their relationship.

'In Italy we have a saying,' Stefano told her dryly as he handed her a plate of food, '*Natale con i tuoi, Pasqua con vuoi*—which roughly translated means, Christmas with the family, Easter with who you like. Food is an important part of the Lucarelli family Christmas. I hope your appetite is healthy.'

But she wasn't part of his family, was she?

Feeling slightly awkward, Liv smiled at his father. 'I hope we're not intruding too much on your celebrations.'

'The biggest celebration is that my son has brought a lovely woman home for Christmas.' He lifted his glass and Stefano said something soft in Italian but the older man simply smiled and drank deeply.

Captivated by his warm, demonstrative family, Liv ate and watched the family dynamics.

Stefano's grandmother was in charge of the kitchen with Isabella and two of the female cousins were also roped in to help.

Liv noticed that one of them—was her name Donatella?—kept casting shy, dreamy looks in Stefano's direction but he didn't seem to notice because he was occupied in an argument with his father which seemed to be about whether or not they should buy an ailing local company.

'No business at the table,' Isabella said sharply, putting plates laden with food in front of them, 'this is Christmas. We don't talk business at Christmas.'

The meal was spectacular and Liv was fascinated by the interaction between everyone at the table. It felt good to be part of a large noisy group. And it was good for Max.

He was seated between Stefano's twin nephews and was happily occupied improving their English.

'We have Father Christmas,' he said solemnly. 'What do you have?'

'*Babo Natale*,' one of the boys said. 'And *La Befana*, she brings us presents in January.'

Suddenly horrified, Max looked at Liv. 'How will Father Christmas know I'm here? What if he takes my presents to our old flat?'

Visibly moved, Isabella put her hand on her heart, murmured something in Italian and then shot out of her seat and hugged Max tightly. 'He will know you are here,' she said firmly. 'We will hang up a sock, yes? And write him a note— in English and Italian just to be sure. Why don't you go and play now? My boys will show you their toys.' Isabella stood up, waved the children away from the table and then glanced at the fire. 'We need another log and that's man's work.' She looked pointedly at her brother and he gave a faint smile and rose to his feet.

'I'll go then, shall I?.' He held out a hand to Liv. 'Come with me. I'll show you the rest of the chalet.'

Liv followed him down two flights of stairs to a basement and then out into the crisp night air. 'I love the smell of wood smoke. And I love your family. You're very lucky.'

'I thought you might be feeling completely overwhelmed.' He hauled her into his arms and curved his hands over her bottom. 'They are noisy and interfering.'

'I think they're lovely. And they love you.' It was exciting, being on her own with him, even if only for a moment. The air was electric and she knew from the glitter in his eyes that he was as aroused as she was. Trying to keep herself in check, she chose a neutral subject. 'Donatella is sweet. She adores you, that's obvious.'

He stilled. 'She's very young,' he said carefully. 'And I'm hoping that she will soon get the message.'

What message? Liv was about to question him further when he brought his mouth down on hers and kissed her hard.

Forgetting everything except the way he made her feel, she kissed him back, oblivious to the cold and the peal of church bells from the village below.

He cared, she thought to herself, her head swimming dizzily. Surely he cared?

Liv woke on Christmas Eve to bright blue skies. Fresh snow had fallen overnight and there was no longer any sign of their footprints of the night before. Branches sagged under the weight of the snow and the valley below them looked as though it had been covered by a thick layer of icing.

Hearing squeals from outside, Liv dressed quickly, relieved that she'd followed Stefano's instructions and purchased some suitable clothes. At some point she was going to have to think about paying him back, but for now she was determined to enjoy the moment.

Pulling on her boots, she stepped outside and saw Max stretching up to put a hat on a large, fat snowman. Isabella and the twins were helping and snow flew through the air with predictable regularity, covering all three boys in soft white clumps.

'Mum, come and see!' Max stamped his boots in the snow and pressed two dark glossy pebbles into the snowman's 'face'. 'Isn't he amazing?'

'We think he looks like Stefano,' Isabella said cheerfully, winking at Liv. 'He always looks grumpy in the mornings.' Leaving the children to finish off the snowman, she wrapped her scarf more firmly round her throat and walked over to Liv. 'Did you sleep?'

'Oh yes.' Liv pushed her hands into her pockets. 'Better than ever before.'

'I always sleep well in the mountains.' Isabella breathed in the cold air and smiled. 'Can I interest you in some serious shopping? Cortina is a shopaholic's paradise, I can assure you.'

Liv shook her head. 'I'd love to see the village but my budget won't stretch to shopping.'

'Stefano will pay,' Isabella said dismissively, knocking snow from the toe of her soft leather boot. 'It's the least he can do given that you've come all this way just to solve his problems.'

Liv looked at her. 'His problems?'

'You must have noticed Donatella.' Isabella rolled her eyes. 'I mean, she can't take her eyes off him. I warned Stefano three weeks ago that she is as much in love with him as ever. To be honest, I even wondered whether he might not come this year, because he hates being cornered by women, but Stefano always finds a solution to everything. Clearly, he decided that bringing you would solve everyone's problems.'

'Really?' Liv's mouth was dry.

'Yes, well…' Isabella looked awkward. 'He did tell me that you'd lost your home. I hope you don't mind. We weren't gos siping or anything—Stefano never gossips. Clearly you've done each other a favour.'

'Yes.' Somehow Liv managed to form the words. 'We have.'

'You're shivering.' Isabella frowned. 'Should we go inside?'

'No. In fact I might go for a walk,' Liv said quickly, buttoning up her coat. 'It's so pretty and I haven't had a chance to take a proper look yet.'

Was it true?

Had he really invited her to spend Christmas with his family just to keep Donatella at a distance?

Isabella seemed about to say something else but there was another snowball fight starting between the children and she hurried across to sort them out.

Taking advantage of the opportunity to escape, Liv walked as quickly as she could up the snow-covered road, suddenly feeling terribly, terribly cold. Although the air was freezing she knew that the chill inside her had more to do with Stefano than the weather.

Why hadn't he told her the truth?

Why had he let her believe that he'd actually wanted her to join him for Christmas?

Why had he let her hope and dream?

She remembered the way Donatella had looked at him and the way that he'd suddenly stilled when she'd mentioned the fact that Donatella clearly liked him.

Oh dear God—she'd been a fool. She'd done it again, taken her dreams and somehow managed to entangle them with reality. She'd turned the world into what she wanted it to be, rather than what it really was.

She'd seen what she'd wanted to see.

Stefano was a man, wasn't he? They'd shared amazing sex

and for him their relationship was nothing more than that. And it wasn't really his fault. *She* was the one who had turned amazing sex into something warmer and deeper. She'd been stupid and careless and—

Blinded by tears, she stumbled into the deep snow at the side of the road and suddenly she just wanted to sink into the cold, white powder and sob. She felt as though she was dying inside and realised that the loss of her dream was much, much more devastating than anything else that had ever happened to her.

'Liv!' Stefano's strong voice carried through the frozen air and Liv stood still, wanting to run but knowing that there was nowhere to run to.

He was wearing sturdy boots, his strong legs were encased in soft fleece trousers and a thick jumper brushed against his darkened jaw. Liv's heart bumped frantically as she watched him approach because he was impossibly, shockingly good-looking and one glance at his face turned her limbs to liquid.

But she shouldn't feel that way, should she?

Not any more.

She felt a flash of desperation. If he came any closer he might see how she felt because she was hopeless at hiding her feelings. She couldn't face him.

But where was she going to go?

With no choice but to wait for him to catch up with her, she took a few deep breaths and told herself that she'd coped with rejection before and she would do it again.

'What are you doing?' His tone was forceful. 'Where are you going?'

Liv concentrated on the snow at her feet. 'For a walk. I needed to be on my own for a while.'

'Why?' His hand closed over hers like a vice. '*Accidenti*, you are as white as a sheet. *What* has happened?'

'Nothing.'

'Nothing doesn't send you stumbling into a snowdrift,' he said grimly, pulling her towards him with firm hands. 'You're upset and I want to know why.'

She felt like too much of a fool to admit the truth. He'd laugh, wouldn't he? He'd laugh if she admitted that she'd thought they shared something more than hot sex. He'd tell her that she was foolish and old-fashioned and that the world just wasn't like that any more.

'I'm just— Nothing.'

Stefano muttered something under his breath in Italian and then took her face in his hands. 'One of the things I love about you is that you are so straightforward and honest. You say what you think and I like that. *Don't* change now. Tell me what's wrong.'

Perhaps if he hadn't used the word 'love' she might have managed to hold it all in, but something pinged inside her and she pulled away, engulfed by an emotion that she couldn't control.

'All right, I'll tell you.' Her breath was coming in rapid pants, as if she'd been running instead of standing still. 'I just—I can't do this. I can't do this any more. The sex was amazing, yes. But I just can't have sex without wanting…more. And I *know* that's my fault, not yours, but I still think you could have been a little bit more honest with me about the reason you invited me here.'

His eyes narrowed. 'Why do you think I invited you here?'

Liv blinked rapidly to clear her vision. 'I *thought* you wanted me to meet your family and then I discover that *actually* you invited me here because you need to keep Donatella at a distance.'

Stefano stilled and his hands dropped to his sides. 'Who told you that?'

'It doesn't matter.' Liv felt a stab of pain that he hadn't denied it. 'And do you know what? The reason we're here shouldn't matter either. It's a beautiful, magical place and Max is having a wonderful time and he's so, so happy playing with your nephews in the snow. I should be relieved and delighted and I *am*, but…' Her words tangled and her emotions raw, she took a breath. 'None of this is your fault. It's me. It's all me. I mean, it should have been obvious to me from the start that our relationship was just about sex, I mean you have…' she waved her hand despairingly '…*all this money*, and what do I have? I live in a tiny flat in a grotty part of London with my son and you live in this flashy apartment with more security than a palace and a lifestyle that makes me drool with envy.'

'Liv—'

'Don't say a word!' Sniffing hard, she lifted a hand to stop him speaking. 'It really isn't your fault that I have fantasies and that I'm basically extremely stupid. You didn't lead me on. You didn't promise me anything. I imagined it all by myself with no help from you. I don't know whether it's the way I'm wired or whether it's because I'm so sensitive about Max, but I just can't seem to do casual relationships. You've been great to Max and without you he would have had a horrible, horrible Christmas and I'll always be grateful to you for that. And now I need to…' She backed away a few steps. 'I need to walk by myself for a bit. Please, please don't follow me.' And without looking at him, she turned and walked up the snowy path as fast as she could without slipping and breaking her neck.

'Mum, he's been! The letter must have worked. He knew I was in Italy and he's brought all my presents here.' Dragging a long, colourful sock behind him Max came charging into her bedroom and Liv sat up and smiled. It was Christmas morning and she was gritty-eyed from lack of sleep and her head felt as though someone was attacking it from the inside with a pick axe.

'That's great, Max.' She glanced towards the window. 'What time is it? Max, it's dark out there!'

'No, it's not. It's snowed again but Stefano says it's going to be a beautiful day and when we've opened our presents he's taking us on a special sleigh ride. It has bells and everything. Are you coming, Mum? The twins and I are going to open our stockings in front of the fire. You don't want to miss it.' Jumping with excitement, he trailed the bulging stocking out of her bedroom and Liv slid out of bed and dressed slowly, knowing that she couldn't avoid seeing Stefano.

When she'd eventually returned to the chalet from her walk on the previous day, there had been no sign of him and Isabella had told her that he'd gone skiing with his father for the day.

So Liv and Max had spent the day with Isabella and her two sons, and her husband had arrived from work in Milan and it had been fun. Together they'd prepared the elaborate Christmas Eve dinner and somehow she'd been so busy that she'd managed to bury her disappointment and her silly fantasies and enjoy herself. His family was warm and demonstrative and at least she hadn't had to look Stefano in the face.

When he and his father had finally returned there had been so much activity and bustle in the chalet that there had been no awkward moments, no intimate opportunities for the two of them to be alone or for him to respond to what she'd said to him in that frozen, solitary moment when she'd bared her soul.

It would be the same today, she told herself as she pulled on the soft cashmere jumper he'd bought her only a few weeks earlier. It would be a busy family day with no opportunity for private moments and then tomorrow they'd be going home to England.

And then she'd rent a flat of her own, forget about Italian millionaires and try and get on with her life.

The next couple of hours passed in a blur of excited squeals, wrapping paper and laughter as everyone passed around presents and Isabella and Stefano's grandmother served breakfast.

Stefano had given Max tickets to see a football match at the famous San Siro stadium in Milan and the little boy was speechless with excitement. 'So we're coming back to Italy? Wow, that is so cool.'

'It's certainly cool,' Isabella agreed cheerfully. 'Minus five today. Make sure you wrap up when you go out.'

Liv glanced at Stefano, grateful that he was obviously intending to carry on spending time with her son and seriously worried as to how she'd be able to maintain a simple friendship with him without making a fool of herself.

Liv handed Max her present to him and found herself with a lump in her throat as he ripped open the paper and found the football boots. 'Oh, Mum…' For a moment he couldn't speak and then he looked at her, eyes shining. 'You're just the best and I love you.' He flung his arms around her and Liv hugged him tightly, reminding herself of what was important in life. She had her lovely, wonderful son and Stefano clearly didn't mean to stop seeing the boy just because they weren't together any more and she was grateful for that. She was lucky. Really lucky.

Max sprinted back to the Christmas tree. 'I've got presents for you and Stefano.' He lifted up two haphazardly wrapped parcels and handed one to Stefano and one to Liv. 'I made them.'

Liv glanced at Stefano, hoping that he wouldn't wince when he saw his present.

He opened it carefully and pulled out a childish drawing of a car.

'It's your Ferrari. I went down to the garage and copied it. That nice security man helped me.' Max watched him anxiously, gauging his reaction. 'I'm not sure I got the nose right.'

Stefano was silent for a moment and then he cleared his throat. 'The nose is perfect,' he said huskily. 'Thank you.'

The fact that he was so careful with Max's feelings somehow made everything seem even worse and Liv dipped her head and concentrated on opening her own present. 'Oh Max…' She lifted the painted pasta necklace from the wrapping. 'It's beautiful.' Slipping it over her head, she smiled at him and his eyes shone with pride.

'Well, you're a girl and Stefano says girls like jewellery and things. He gave you earrings and that thing for your hair, but he didn't give you a necklace.' Max slid his arms round her and Liv hugged him tightly.

'I love it. It's really beautiful.' She watched with a lump in her throat while the twins ripped the paper off their presents and then Isabella tilted her head.

'I hear bells outside—did anyone order a sleigh?'

Stefano rose to his feet. 'We'll see you later. Don't eat lunch without us.'

'Isn't everyone coming?' As Liv slipped her arms into her coat, she glanced around her but the group was already breaking up and doing different things. Donatella was going skiing with the other cousins, Isabella was joining her grandmother in the kitchen to prepare the meal.

Max was speechless with delight when he saw the horse-drawn sleigh waiting on the snowy path outside the chalet. 'We're going to ride in that?'

'You certainly are.' Stefano scooped him up and deposited

him in the back of the sleigh on a deep pile of sheepskin rugs and soft cushions. Following more slowly, Liv climbed up beside him, horribly conscious that it was just the three of them.

She really didn't want to be alone with Stefano. But what choice did she have? If she made an excuse, she'd spoil Max's fun and she didn't want to do that. So she said nothing and tried to look as though this was her idea of a perfect trip.

And in different circumstances it probably would have been.

The driver urged the horses forward and the sleigh moved smoothly along the snowy track that snaked up the mountain through tall pine trees. The only sounds were the muffled thud of horses' hooves, the creak of the oiled leather harness and the tinkle of sleigh bells.

Just enjoy the moment, Liv told herself desperately, and then she glanced at Max's face and felt herself soften with love. She would have been willing to face a thousand demons if it meant seeing her little boy smile the way he was smiling right now.

'It's magical,' she murmured and Stefano spread a blanket over her knees.

'Magical and freezing. Are you cold?'

'No.' *How could she be cold when he was so close?* Reminding herself not to get any ideas, Liv shrank back against the soft cushions and concentrated on the view.

The pain of not being with him would fade in time, wouldn't it?

And if it didn't, she'd somehow learn to live with it.

Max peered ahead of them, oblivious to the tension between the adults and fascinated by the horses. 'Can they go faster? Can we gallop? Can I help to drive them?'

'No, to all those questions,' Stefano said dryly, his eyes amused as he watched the child. 'We don't want to end up at the bottom of the valley. I think, for now, we'll leave the driving to the expert.'

'It was kind of you to do this for him.' Liv risked a glance and then looked away quickly, appalled by the sudden stab of need that swamped her.

'I didn't do it for him.' Stefano's voice was soft. 'I did it for myself. Because it's the only way to escape from my enormous family. Families can give you many things, but not privacy and peace and quiet. I can't quite believe that I've resorted to hiring a horse and sleigh, but that should give you some indication of how desperate I am.'

Desperate?

'Don't lean that far out, Max.' Anxious about safety, Liv reached out a hand and pulled the child back and then glanced at Stefano. 'Why do you need privacy?'

'Because I refuse to propose to you with my entire family watching.'

There was a long silence and Liv sat absolutely still, unable to speak or move, sure that she'd misheard him. He couldn't possibly have said what she thought he'd just said. She recited his words back to herself in her head. Then she turned her head slowly and their eyes met and held. 'What did you say?'

'What you thought I said. Marry me, Liv.' The look in his eyes made her body tingle and warm.

'Stefano—'

'*Te amo.* I love you. I should have told you that days ago and I'm sorry I didn't, but until yesterday I wasn't sure you'd say yes.'

'You should have asked me,' Max chipped in breathlessly. 'I could have told you she'd say yes. She's always staring at you and looking goopy and she smiles *all* the time, especially when you've just said something to her.'

Liv blushed, amazed that Max had noticed so much.

Stefano laughed, but his eyes didn't leave Liv's face for a moment. '*What* is "goopy"? This is not a word I know.'

'It's sort of...' Max pulled a face and shuddered as he tried to explain. 'Girly. I had to marry one of the girls in my class in a play this term and it was the grossest thing that has ever happened to me. She looked as though she was going to *eat* me or something. And she said lots of mushy stuff. If Mum marries you do we get to live in your cool apartment and play with all the gadgets?'

A wry smile on his face, Stefano spoke to the driver in Italian and the sleigh immediately glided to a halt.

The horses snorted and tossed their heads, their breath clouding the freezing air, their hooves making a muffled sound as they stamped the snowy ground.

'How would you like to exchange a few words with the horses, Max?' Stefano lifted the little boy down from the sleigh and Max eagerly sprinted forward to stroke the horses.

Beneath them lay the valley. Smoke curled upwards from chimneys, snow sparkled in the bright sunshine and the mountains rose up with pride, dominating the breathtaking landscape with their stark, wild beauty. Breathing in the crisp cold air and the scent of pine trees, Liv knew that she'd never forget this moment as long as she lived. 'You love me?'

'I love you. Do you want me to say it again?' Stefano took her face in his hands and looked at her, his dark eyes serious. 'I love you, *tesoro*.'

Her heart was thumping and her mouth was dry. 'But...' She swallowed hard. 'I'm no one.'

Stefano gave a slow smile that turned him from handsome to devastating. 'You're the woman I'm going to marry.'

She felt dizzy and shaky. *Marry?* 'I thought—I thought that for you it was just sex,' Liv whispered. 'I wanted it to be more. I really, really wanted it to be more, but that was all in my own head.'

'It wasn't in your head.' His eyes were gentle on hers. 'It was real. And it wasn't just sex.'

'But...you didn't say anything.'

'Liv, you haven't been with a man for four years.' He spoke the words quietly, just for her. 'I know what a big thing this is for you, even more so because you have always put your son's needs before your own. To begin with you rejected everything I gave you. You were *so* independent. I was giving you time to get used to the idea of being with me. That's why I wanted you to come home with me for Christmas.'

'When you first invited me I was so excited. I thought it meant that you cared, but then Isabella told me that you wanted to keep Donatella at a distance—'

'So it was Isabella.' His eyes narrowed wrathfully. 'Remind me to drop my sister in a snowdrift later. Liv, you're an intelligent woman. Do I look as though I need help keeping women at a distance?'

Liv bit her lip, her eyes scanning every detail of his handsome face. 'I suppose by now you must be pretty experienced at managing the expectations of the opposite sex.'

A smile touched the corners of his mouth. 'I have had some practice, I admit. But this isn't about me, is it, *tesoro*? It's about you.' His eyes held hers, demanding her full attention. 'You still don't believe that you are lovable and sexy. You are so lacking in confidence that when someone suggests I might have had an ulterior motive for bringing you here, you don't even question it.'

Dragging her gaze from his, Liv realised that her heart was pounding. 'Stefano—'

Strong fingers caught her chin and he forced her to look at him again. 'I'm going to make you see yourself as others see you, Liv. Warm, beautiful, talented, clever and a wonderful mother. And sexy.' He drew her head towards his and his eyes glittered dark with sexual promise. 'Very, very sexy. I have never brought a woman here before. What does that say to you?'

Hypnotised, Liv stared up at him and he slowly brought his mouth down to hers.

'It says that I'm crazy about you,' he murmured against her lips. 'It says that I cannot bear to be without you, even for a few days. That is why I brought you here, *tesoro*. And I wanted to see how you coped with my family.' He pulled back slightly, a sardonic gleam in his eyes. 'As you've already gathered, being with me comes with a great deal of family interference. Do you think you can stand it?'

Still in a state of suspended disbelief, Liv couldn't think properly. 'I— Does your father know that—? What if he doesn't approve? I have a child, Stefano. Donatella would probably be a far more suitable Italian wife.'

'Donatella and I would drive each other mad in less than a day. She isn't the right woman for me.' He sat back in his seat, his arm draped along the back of the carriage, very much his own man. 'You, on the other hand, enchant me and fascinate me and have done since the first moment I saw you hugging Anna.'

'That was so embarrassing—'

'I heard her say that she wanted to buy you hot sex for Christmas and you looked so appalled that I was instantly intrigued. A woman like you should be having hot sex every night of her life.'

Liv blushed. 'You were *so* kind to me. That night the car broke down and then with my flat—'

'It wasn't kindness, Liv.' Stefano slid his arm round her and curved her against him. 'I've never felt so protective towards a woman. I don't know what happens to me when I'm with you but I just want to wrap you up and keep you safe.'

His words brought a lump to her throat. 'Stefano—'

'I make you this promise, *tesoro*,' he said huskily, 'I won't let you be hurt ever again if it is in my power to prevent it. I won't let you struggle and I won't let you make any more sacrifices.'

His words drove the last of the breath from her quivering body. The emotions inside her swelled to a point that she could barely contain them. When had anyone ever taken care of her before? She'd always had to do it herself. On her own. She'd fought, struggled and worried her way through parenthood, with no one to share the burden. And now this man was telling her that she no longer had anything to worry about. She was afraid to move in case the dream shattered into a million tiny fragments.

'I thought it was because you felt sorry for me.'

'It was because I was falling in love with you. Almost from that first moment. You're very easy to love.'

Tears pricked her eyes and her throat felt full. 'This sort of thing doesn't happen to me.'

'Yes, it does. It's happening now.' He was smiling and Liv shook her head, the tears blurring her vision.

'No. It doesn't—and I can't…' She brushed her hand across her face. 'Any moment now you're going to tell me this is a joke.'

'Then perhaps this will convince you.' Stefano reached into his pocket and pulled out a tiny silver box. 'I went out yesterday and bought this for you.'

'Yesterday? But you were skiing…' Her voice cracked and she stared at the box, wondering whether it was real or whether her mind had conjured up this whole situation.

'I was choosing a ring suitable for my future wife. I knew it had to be something extremely special because *she* is extremely special.' Stefano flicked open the box and a huge diamond solitaire winked and flashed in the winter sunlight

Liv gave a gasp of shock and then lifted her eyes to his 'It's…a ring. You bought me a ring.'

'You're right.' His eyes laughed into hers. 'It's a ring. It' tradition for the man to give his woman a ring when he' proposing.'

She could hardly breathe. 'You want to marry me.'

'That's what I've been saying for the past five minutes. Stefano's gaze flickered briefly to the front of the sleigh. ' hate to hurry this romantic moment, but Max is going to ge bored with those horses shortly and then the goopy, mush stuff is going to have to finish.'

'Your father—'

'My father loves you, but even if he didn't it wouldn' make a difference. He's not the one marrying you. I am.'

'You are?' She looked at him, unable to believe that lif could transform from misery to perfect pleasure in such short time. 'But yesterday, when I told you how I felt—'

'I was so stunned by what you said that I didn't even sto you walking away. But you did me a favour. I realised tha there was no point in holding back and giving you time t adjust to the fact that we were together. I could see that word alone wouldn't be enough to convince you that I love you.'

Hardly daring to breathe, Liv gazed at the glittering diamon and then at him. 'Stefano, you couldn't have found a woma with less to offer you. I don't have any money at all and—'

'Fortunately I have more than enough for both of us.' Hi possessive gaze was fixed on her in blatant appreciation an she felt herself blushing.

'Don't look at me like that.'

'I'm going to be looking at you like that for the next fifty years at least, *tesoro*,' he drawled softly, 'so you'd better get used to it.'

Liv lifted a hand to her throat. 'I want to be with you more than anything, you know that. But I can't marry you.'

His dark eyes narrowed ominously. '*Liv*—'

'*How can I marry you?* I don't have a single penny in my bank account and you're a multi-millionaire. You've bought me a ring that must have cost more than I earn in a year! It's very easy for you to dismiss that, but it matters! If I marry you, you'll think I'm a gold-digger,' she said passionately and when he started to roar with laughter she glared at him in exasperation. 'Why is that funny?'

'Because for a moment I really thought you were refusing me,' he gasped through his laughter, 'and having never proposed to a woman before, you might have done irreparable harm to my arrogance and my ego.'

'I'm being serious, Stefano.'

'So am I. Fortunately for both of us, I have considerable experience with gold-diggers, *tesoro*. Believe me, you don't have any of the necessary qualifications.'

'You don't understand. I like the fact that you have money,' Liv said honestly, watching for his reaction with something close to dread, afraid that she might drive him away. '*I like the money, Stefano!* I like the fact that you don't have to worry about paying bills. I like the fact you can just wave your credit card, snap your fingers and solve a million problems. I even like being given diamond earrings and beautiful clothes! There. Does that shock you?'

'Liv, you've been counting every penny for the past four years. It's entirely natural that having access to money should come as a relief. To not like the money would make you stupid, no? And you *certainly* are not stupid.' He was watching her with a considerable degree of amusement in his eyes. 'Just enjoy it. Why are you worrying?'

'Because I'm afraid you'll think my feelings for you are tied up with the money.'

Stefano smiled and took her face in his hands. 'Liv, I've always known what your feelings for me are, *tesoro*. Fortunately for me, you aren't experienced enough to hide them. I can even describe the moment when you first realised that you loved me.'

Her eyes widened. 'You can?'

'Of course. It was when you woke up in my bed the morning after the ball.'

'Oh.' Liv gave a shocked laugh. 'How can you be so confident about everything?'

'Because, unlike you, no one has ever dented my self esteem.' Bending his head, he kissed her gently, his mouth lingering against hers. 'I love the fact that you can't hide your feelings. I also love your kindness, your honesty, your total selflessness, your amazing confidence and skill at work, your sense of humour, your incredibly sexy body—'

'Stop!' Laughing, Liv shook her head and pulled away slightly. 'That's not me you're describing. I'm not used to so many compliments.'

'Then get used to it because there is no end of compliment coming your way, *tesoro*.' Gently, Stefano stroked her flushed cheek with the backs of his fingers then he lifted the ring out of the velvet case. 'Stop worrying about the money and enjoy it. Given that my life is about to become your life, it would be a little complicated if you didn't like the money.'

He really wanted to marry her?

It was too much to absorb. 'I can't believe this is happening.' Liv stared at the beautiful ring in his hand. Her heart was pounding, her legs were shaking and she didn't know whether to laugh or cry. 'I've shut myself away for so long. That first night when you took me to that Italian restaurant, I just wanted to shrink into the woodwork.'

'I had a good time, but you had absolutely *no* confidence.'

'It had been ages since I'd been out with a man and I had no idea what to say. I was worried that you were terribly bored.'

'You have never bored me,' Stefano breathed, 'and I couldn't believe that you hadn't been with a man for so long.'

'I just wasn't interested,' she admitted, checking that Max was still patting the horses. 'I suppose I was terrified of rejection. Anna despaired of me, but I honestly couldn't imagine wanting to have sex ever again. Then I met you and sex with you was so amazing that suddenly I couldn't imagine living without it. You've turned me into a sex maniac.'

With a husky laugh, Stefano took her hand in his and slid the ring onto her finger. 'Then the sooner we are married, the better. I am willing to sacrifice myself by marrying a sex maniac,' he said dryly, 'just as long as there is no confusion as to whose woman you are.'

Liv stared down at the diamond that sparkled on her finger. 'It's stunning.'

'It tells the world that you are mine.' Stefano gave a satisfied smile and Liv tore her eyes away from the ring, a lump building in her throat as she looked up at him.

'What can I ever give you in return?'

'Love, *tesoro*.' His hands strong and confident, he drew her against him. 'You're giving me love, and that's a gift beyond price.'

'Yuck!' Max scrambled up beside them. 'Did she say no or something?'

Still sniffing, Liv pulled out of Stefano's arms. 'I said yes, Max.'

'So why are you crying?'

'Because I'm happy.'

Max stared at her bemused and then exchanged a look with Stefano, man to man. 'She cries when she's sad and she cries when she's happy. Girls are so confusing, aren't they?'

'Very confusing.' With a smile, Stefano released Liv and lifted the child onto his lap. 'How would you fancy coming to live with me, Max?'

'For ever?'

'Yes, for ever.'

Liv couldn't help it. The tears were pouring down her face and she turned her head and buried her face in Stefano's sleeve, feeling like a complete idiot and so deliriously happy that she wanted to dance with joy.

Max was concentrating on the important issues. 'Will we live in your apartment?'

'To start with. But then I thought we might look around for a nice big house. We need a garden so that we can have a goal.'

'My own goal?' Max bounced on his lap and Stefano winced.

'I hope you didn't want more children,' he muttered under his breath, and Liv started to laugh because her life suddenly seemed so amazing and everything around her was just perfect.

'Can we go and get married straight away in case you change your mind?'

'He won't change his mind.' Max settled himself between them. 'Stefano was lonely until we came along. He had no Christmas decorations of his own, can you believe that? Now he has us, we'll be able to help him with his Christmas tree every year. And you'll be able to sleep in his bed, like married people are supposed to.'

The sleigh bells jangled as the horses moved back up the road towards the chalet and Liv and Stefano exchanged a look over the top of his head.

'I love you, Stefano.' Saying the words suddenly made it all seem real and she suddenly discovered that it was perfectly possible to smile and cry at the same time. 'I love you *so much* and this is the best Christmas I could possibly have imagined.'

His dark eyes flared with emotion. 'And I love you, *tesoro*. You're mine. Always.'

'Oh please!' Giggling and squirming between them, Max covered his ears and shuddered. 'Someone let me out of here before I'm sick. I'm sure Father Christmas doesn't have to listen to this in *his* sleigh.'

TWO SPARKLING CHRISTMAS ROMANCES...

...full of the joys and warmth of the season

Twelfth Night Proposal
by Karen Rose Smith

Rescued by the Magic of Christmas
by Melissa McClone

Available 7th November 2008

Celebrate 100 years of pure reading pleasure with Mills & Boon®

To mark our centenary, each month we're publishing a special 100th Birthday Edition. These celebratory editions are packed with extra features and include a FREE bonus story.

Plus, you have the chance to enter a fabulous monthly prize draw. See 100th Birthday Edition books for details.

Now that's worth celebrating!

September 2008
Crazy about her Spanish Boss by Rebecca Winters
Includes FREE bonus story
Rafael's Convenient Proposal

November 2008
The Rancher's Christmas Baby
by Cathy Gillen Thacker
Includes FREE bonus story *Baby's First Christmas*

December 2008
One Magical Christmas by Carol Marinelli
Includes FREE bonus story *Emergency at Bayside*

Look for Mills & Boon® 100th Birthday Editions at your favourite bookseller or visit
www.millsandboon.co.uk

FREE

4 BOOKS AND A SURPRISE GIFT!

We would like to take this opportunity to thank you for reading this Mills & Boon® book by offering you the chance to take FOUR more specially selected titles from the Medical™ series absolutely FREE! We're also making this offer to introduce you to the benefits of the Mills & Boon® Book Club—

- ★ **FREE home delivery**
- ★ **FREE gifts and competitions**
- ★ **FREE monthly Newsletter**
- ★ **Books available before they're in the shops**
- ★ **Exclusive Mills & Boon® Book Club offers**

Accepting these FREE books and gift places you under no obligation to buy; you may cancel at any time, even after receiving your free shipment. Simply complete your details below and return the entire page to the address below. You don't even need a stamp!

YES! Please send me 4 free Medical books and a surprise gift. I understand that unless you hear from me, I will receive 6 superb new titles every month for just £2.99 each, postage and packing free. I am under no obligation to purchase any books and may cancel my subscription at any time. The free books and gift will be mine to keep in any case.

M8ZEE

Ms/Mrs/Miss/Mr...Initials ....

BLOCK CAPITALS PLEASE

Surname ....

Address ....

....

....Postcode ....

Send this whole page to:
The Mills & Boon Book Club, FREEPOST CN81, Croydon, CR9 3WZ